THE BRIDE'S BABY OF SHAME

THE BRIDE'S BABY OF SHAME

CAITLIN CREWS

MILLS & BOON

First published in Great Britain 2018
by Mills & Boon, an imprint of HarperCollins*Publishers*
1 London Bridge Street, London, SE1 9GF

Large Print edition 2018

ISBN: 978-0-263-07432-1

MIX
Paper from
responsible sources
FSC® C007454

This book is produced from independently certified FSC™ paper to ensure responsible forest management. For more information visit www.harpercollins.co.uk/green.

Printed and bound in Great Britain
by CPI Group (UK) Ltd, Croydon, CR0 4YY

This book is dedicated to the memory of
the best Christmas afternoon tea ever with
our editors Megan Haslam and Flo Nicoll
in London, where Jane and I
came up with the idea for this duet.
And then had so much fun writing it!

CHAPTER ONE

RENZO CRISANTI LOATHED ENGLAND.

He was no fan of great, sprawling London, choking on commuters and tourists and lumbering red buses wherever he turned. He disliked the countryside, oppressively green and ever damp. He preferred his native Sicily, its mountains and sweeping Mediterranean views. England was too dour and grim for a man who had gone from the colorful streets of his hometown to a career racing impossibly fast cars all over the planet.

He might have retired from racing, but that didn't change the fact that he was a Sicilian. In his opinion, that made him the best of Italy plus that little bit extra—and it meant he was fundamentally unsuited to what the English called their summer.

Even on an evening like tonight in late June, the English sky was wringing itself out, much colder and rainier than it ought to have been in Renzo's estimation.

He preferred his own small village in the mountains outside Taormina at this time of year. A warmer sea in the distance and a happier sun to go along with the sweep of all that history, with Mount Etna rising in all her glory above it all.

Instead, he found himself just outside Winchester, England, winding in and around rolling hills so far out into the countryside that there was hardly any light. There had been a towering cathedral rising up over the medieval city, but still, Renzo preferred the battered, ageless wilderness of the Sicilian countryside to all this manicured charm. He'd felt hemmed in as he'd driven through the Winchester city center before heading out to the surrounding fields.

He wished he'd followed his initial knee-jerk reaction to this whole situation weeks ago.

Because Renzo had known Sophie Carmichael-Jones was nothing but trouble the moment he'd laid eyes on her.

Steer clear, something had whispered inside him the moment he'd seen her, like a kick in the gut.

But he'd paid that foreboding voice no mind.

Renzo had been in Monaco for the annual motor race, though not as a driver. He'd stopped racing while he was ahead and still in one piece several years back, and had channeled his notoriety into a line of clubs, a few select hotels dotted around Europe, and a vineyard back in Sicily. And where better than Monaco to advertise to the very high-class, European clientele he hoped to serve? He'd been enjoying a drink with some friends when he'd happened to look up and see her.

She had glowed. That was the first thing he'd noticed, as if she'd walloped him with all that shine. She'd worn a metallic gown that had been perfectly demure on its own, but that hadn't been the source of all that *light*. That had come straight from her.

Renzo was no stranger to beautiful women. They flocked to him and he, in turn, considered himself something of a connoisseur. But this one… Her dark hair had been pulled back with a certain insouciance, only a few tendrils escaping and showing the faintest hint of a deep copper beneath the lights. Her lips had been painted siren red, her brows were dark, and she'd worn large, gleaming earrings that Renzo had known in an instant were real despite their size. She'd looked elegant. Chic. Endless legs that suggested a certain coltishness and that lovely, inescapably aristocratic face.

But her eyes, brown and shot through with gold, had been so sad.

Their gazes had collided, there on the floor of the Casino de Monte Carlo. Renzo had lost his train of thought. Not something that often happened to a man who'd made his name and his first fortune thanks to his singular focus and steady hands.

He'd stood up from his table, crossed the floor, and found himself standing before her without knowing he'd meant to move.

He had been aware of everything about her, there in the middle of a crowd that he'd hardly noticed. She'd caught her breath. He'd seen color high on her cheeks. And he'd known that the chemistry he could feel, electric and intense, was affecting her, too.

It was insanity.

"You must tell me two things," he'd told her, feeling as if they were all alone when he knew full well that they were not. That half of Europe stood arrayed around them. He couldn't seem to bring himself to care. "One, your name. And two, why you are so sad. This is Monte Carlo, *cara*. Nothing but joy is permitted."

"I'm not sad at all," she'd said after a moment, and somehow, he hadn't been surprised that she was English, though she'd spoken to him in the same Italian he'd used. Just with that unmistakable accent. "That would require far more emotion than the situation warrants. A better description is *resigned*."

"You are far too young and much too beautiful for resignation."

Her lovely lips had curved, and Renzo had wanted nothing more than to taste that red-slicked smile. Then, there. He wasn't fussy.

"While you strike me as far too sophisticated for such idle flattery," she'd replied.

Renzo had been in the grip of a fever. Looking back, that was the only explanation. He'd reached over and taken her hand in his—

And they'd both breathed a little heavily at the contact.

He'd been aware of his own heartbeat, intense and demanding. He'd seen her pulse, there in the column of her neck, drumming out the same insistent rhythm. He would never know how he had restrained himself from leaning over and covering it with his mouth.

It had been as if they'd made lightning between them, such wild electricity he marveled the whole of Monaco didn't burst into flames. It was as if their skin could scarcely contain it.

Renzo had known then and there that he would be inside this beautiful stranger within the hour.

Or die trying.

"Let me try this, then," he had said, casting aside his customary charm for the urgency the moment appeared to warrant. "I need you, *cara.* I don't care who you are or what you had planned tonight. I want you. I want to taste every part of you again and again, until I would know you in the blackest night. I want to taste you in my mouth. I want everything—and then I want to do it again. And again. Until there's nothing left of either one of us."

"I don't believe in immolation," she'd said, though her voice was hoarse.

"You will."

She had shuddered. She had swayed slightly on

her feet. She shot a look over her shoulder, somewhere through the crowd, then had returned her attention to him.

He could read her need and better yet, her surrender, all over her face.

Renzo had wasted no time. He took her hand in his and led her to the private exit, where he could retrieve his car without any interference from fans or photographers. In moments, they'd been speeding away, up into the hills toward the villa he maintained far above glittering Monaco and the Côte d'Azur spread out below.

"I am Renzo Crisanti," he had told her, because there was something in him that needed her to know him, whatever that meant. Whatever came next. "And, *bellissima*, you still haven't told me your name."

She had shifted beside him, all sleek lines and the quiet, humming intensity of her considerable beauty—so much like the cars he loved and handled the same way he intended to handle her.

With all his skill and focus. With all the acute ferocity that had propelled him to the top of his profession.

There was a reason Renzo had never had a

crash. And he didn't plan to change his record that night, not even for this mysterious woman who'd already had him tight and hard and greedy when all he'd had of her was a brief touch of her hand.

It was as if he'd never had another woman in his life.

"You can call me Elizabeth," she'd said.

It was the first lie she'd told him, Renzo thought now, trying to tamp down his temper. But it was nowhere near the last.

He pulled his car over to the side of the road, near what looked like an abandoned old croft—or whatever it was they called their falling-down sheds in this part of England. He cut the engine and unfolded himself from the low-slung sports car, adjusting the ends of the driving gloves he wore out of habit as he stood there beside the vehicle and attempted to access his usual, legendary calm. The motor made its noises, as if protesting that he'd cut the drive short. The summer rain had let off, but the night was still cool. Renzo flipped up the collar of his leather jacket against the pervasive damp and checked his watch, impatient.

And perhaps something a good deal more intense than merely impatient, if he was honest.

Because he had a score to settle with the woman he was meeting here, off in the middle of nowhere, so late at night in a foreign country.

As if he was answering a summons. As if he, Renzo Crisanti, were so malleable and easily led he would travel across the whole of Europe for a woman he had already bedded.

His fingers stung and he released them, unaware he'd clenched his hands into fists at his sides.

At first he thought it was just a shadow, moving rapidly down the hill from one of England's grand old houses in the distance. The directions she'd sent had been explicit. This country lane to that little byway, skirting around the edges of stately manors and rolling fields lined in hedgerows. But the more he watched, his eyes adjusting to the inky dark, the more he recognized the figure approaching him as Sophie.

Sophie, who'd given Renzo her innocence without thinking to warn him.

Sophie, who had called herself Elizabeth on that long, hot, and impossibly carnal night in Monaco.

Sophie, who had lied to him. To *him*.

Sophie, who had sneaked away while he slept, leaving him with nothing—not even her real name—until she'd chosen to reveal it in the most humiliating way possible, in a hastily mailed newspaper clipping.

Of Sophie Elizabeth Carmichael-Jones, daughter of a wealthy and titled British family, who was engaged to marry an earl.

Sophie, *his* Sophie, who would be another man's wife in the morning.

Renzo's jaw ached. He forced himself to unclench his teeth, and his fists again, while he was at it. He was a man known far and wide for the boneless, lazy manner with which he conducted both his business and his pleasure. It was his trademark.

It was a mask he had carefully cultivated to hide the truth—that he was a true Sicilian in every sense of the term, especially when it came to the volcanic temper he'd spent his life learning to keep under strict control.

This woman made him a stranger to himself.

She skidded a bit on the wet grass at the bottom of the hill, then righted herself. And her swift, indrawn breath as she started toward him seemed to crack through him like thunder.

There were no lights out here, lost somewhere in

England's greenest hills, for his sins—but Renzo could see her perfectly. He'd meant what he'd told her in Monte Carlo.

He would know her if he was blind.

Her stride. Her scent. The particular way she held her head. The little sound of erotic distress she made in the back of her throat when he—

But this was not the time for such things. Not when there was so much to discuss, and her with the wedding of the year in the morning.

She was wearing a simple pair of leggings tucked into high boots and what looked like long-sleeved shirts, layered one on top of the other. Her clothes molded themselves to her trim figure and showed off the sleek, sweet curve of her behind and those long, long legs he'd had wrapped around his shoulders while he'd thrust deep inside her and made them both groan. Her dark chestnut hair fell down all around her, looking like a soft black curtain in the darkness.

She stopped before him, and for a moment, all he could think about was that night. She'd been sitting naked in his bed, laughing at something he'd said while she'd piled her hair on the top of her head and had tied it in a knot.

So simple. So unconsciously alluring. Then, and now when he knew better.

So devious, he reminded himself harshly.

But what he remembered most was that he'd had her three times by then.

It was a hunger he couldn't contain, couldn't reason away, couldn't even douse afterward when he'd wanted to think of other things. It had been weeks and yet here it was again, as voracious and as greedy as it had been that night in Monaco.

Worse, perhaps, because he had tasted her. Because he knew exactly what he was missing.

Renzo thought he likely vibrated with his need for her, only now it made him as darkly furious as it did hard.

"Renzo..."

She said his name quietly, tipping her head back so she could look him in the eye.

And if her eyes were sad, or resigned, or anything else at all, he told himself he didn't care.

"How nice to see you again, Sophie," he said in English, a language they had never spoken to each other.

He saw her shudder at the sound, but he forged

on, unwilling to permit himself to do anything but what he'd come here to do.

Which was make her pay.

"Please accept my deepest congratulations on your upcoming wedding. I read all about it in the papers," he drawled, flint and rage and no mask to hide it. "Tomorrow, is it not?"

Sophie felt sick.

She wanted to blame it on the shocking news she'd gotten two days ago at her doctor's office, but she knew better.

It wasn't the mistake she'd made or the person she now had to accept she was because of it.

It wasn't the miraculous little accident that was growing inside her, whether she believed it or not. The accident that was proof that those stolen hours in Monaco hadn't been a dream, after all—that what had happened between her and this startlingly handsome stranger had been real. It was something she could cling to no matter how much of a mess she found herself in now.

But that wasn't what had her stomach in knots tonight.

No. It was the way Renzo was looking at her.

As if he hated her.

Which was fair enough. Sophie wasn't too fond of herself at the moment, now she knew the truth about the headaches she'd been having the past week or so, and that oddly *thick* sensation that wasn't quite nausea—

But Sophie wasn't sure she could bear it. Not from him.

Her distant father, more calculator than human, was one thing. Her even more remote and disinterested fiancé another.

But Renzo was the only thing in her life that had never been a part of this grim little march toward fulfilling the sacred duty that she'd been told was her responsibility since her birth. Every single part of her life had been orchestrated to lead directly and triumphantly toward her wedding tomorrow. She had been raised on dire warnings about the perils of shirking her obligations to her family and endless stories about the many ancestors who would rise from their vaults in protest should any hint of a scandal taint their name.

There had never been any light. Or hope. Or anything like heat.

Sophie was so *cold*. Always and forever frozen solid, no matter the weather.

Because she'd been aware since she was very small that the sorts of things that warmed a body—strong spirits, wild passion, scandalously revealing garments of any kind—were not permitted for the Carmichael-Jones heiress.

She was to be without stain. Virginal and pure until she handed herself over to her husband, a man chosen by her father before she could walk.

Because the world kept turning ever closer to a marvelous future, but Sophie had been raised in the past. The deep, dark past, where her father didn't condescend to ignore her wishes—Sophie had been raised to know better than to express one. Even to herself.

Everything had been ice, always.

So Sophie had made herself its queen.

But Renzo had been all the light and hope and heat she'd given up believing was possible, packed into that one long, glorious night.

Every wild, impetuous summer Sophie had ever missed out on. Every burning hot streak of strong drink she'd never permitted herself to taste. Every dessert she'd refused, lest her figure be seen as anything but perfectly trim while clad in the finest couture, the better to reflect both wealthy families of which she was the unwilling emblem.

Renzo had been lazy laughter and impossible fire, intense and overwhelming, vast and uncontainable and so much *more* than she'd been ready for that she still woke in the night in a rush, her heart pounding, as if he was touching her again—

"Why am I here?"

He sounded impatient. Bored, even. Something in her recoiled instantly, because she knew that particular tone of voice. Her father used it. So did her fiancé. They were busy, serious men with no time for the frothy, insubstantial concerns of the woman they traded between them like so much chattel.

She wasn't a *person*, that tone of voice told her. She was made of contracts and property, the distribution of wealth and the expectations of others. Hers wasn't a *life*, it was a list of obligations and hefty consequences if she failed to meet each one.

The old Sophie would have slunk off, duly chastened. She would never have come out here in the first place.

But that Sophie was gone, burned to a crisp in Monaco. Forever ruined, in every sense of the term.

This Sophie tried to find her spine, and then straightened it.

"You contacted me."

"Is that the game you wish to play, *cara*?" Renzo lifted an indolent shoulder, then dropped it. "You sent me newspaper clippings of your engagement. The wedding of the year, I am to understand. A thousand felicitations, of course. Your fiancé is a lucky man indeed."

Sophie didn't particularly care for the way he looked at her as he said that, but she was too busy reeling to respond to it.

"Newspaper clippings…?"

But even as she asked the question, she knew.

She hadn't sent Renzo anything. It wouldn't have occurred to her, no matter how many times she woke in the night with his taste in her mouth. But she knew someone who would have.

Poppy.

Dear, darling Poppy, Sophie's best friend from their school days. Romantic, dreamy Poppy, who wanted nothing but happiness for Sophie.

And who had never seemed to understand that for all Sophie's advantages, and she knew they were many, *happiness* was never on offer.

"Don't be tiresome, my dear," her mother had sighed years ago, when Sophie, trembling, had dared to ask why her own choices were never given the slightest bit of consideration. "*Choice* is a word that poor people use because they have nothing else. You do. Try being grateful, not greedy."

Sophie had tried. And over the years she'd stopped longing for things she knew she could never have.

That wasn't Poppy's way.

"You demanded I meet you here," Renzo was saying, a different sort of laziness in his voice then. This one had an edge. "And so, naturally, I placed my entire life on hold at such a summons and raced to your side like a well-trained hound."

He made a show of looking around, but there was nothing for miles but fields and hedges. No prying eyes. No concerned relatives who would claim to their dying day they only had Sophie's best interests at heart.

The stately house where her wedding was to be

held in the morning was over the next hill and Sophie, who had never sneaked anywhere in her life before that night in Monaco, had felt a sickening combination of daring and scared as she'd crept out of her room and run from the hall tonight.

It was pathetic, really.

How had she lived twenty-six long years and failed to recognize how sad and small her life really was?

Renzo wasn't finished. "Now that we're both caught up, perhaps you can tell me why I've been called upon to take part in this latest episode of what appears to be a rather melodramatic and messy life?"

Sophie swallowed. The words *melodramatic* and *messy* had never applied to her life. Not ever. Not until she'd met him. She opened her mouth to speak, but nothing came out.

That was the real story of her life.

Her heart was beating so loudly she couldn't understand how Renzo didn't hear it.

His mouth moved, then, but she would never call that a smile. Then he made it worse, reaching over to take her chin in his firm hand, the buttery leather of the gloves he wore only highlighting the intensity of his grip.

And it was the same inside her as it had always been, gloves or no.

Fire.

"What lies will you tell me tonight, I wonder?" he asked, low and dark. Ominous.

"You found me," Sophie said, trying to keep her feet solid beneath her. Trying to ignore the wildfire heat ignited in her. Again. "I… I didn't want…"

She didn't know how to do this.

He had texted her out of nowhere, as far as she'd known.

This is Renzo. You must want to meet.

Now, standing outside on a cool, wet night, Sophie had to ask herself what she thought he had been offering, exactly. Blackmail?

That was what she'd told herself. That was why she'd come.

But she understood, now that he was touching her again, that she'd been lying to herself.

And now she had to lie to him. Again.

The trouble was, Sophie had never told so many

lies before in her life. What would be the point? Too many people knew too much about her, and everyone was more than happy to compare notes and then decide what was in her best interest without her input. Therefore, she'd always done exactly what was expected of her. She'd done well at school because her father had made it clear that she was expected to be more than simply an ornament.

"Clever conversation and sparkling wit are not something one is either born with or not, Sophie," her father had told her when she'd been barely thirteen. "They're weapons in an arsenal and I expect you to be an excellent shot."

Sophie had made certain she was. After school, she'd involved herself with only carefully vetted charities, so as never to cause her father or future husband any cause for concern about what she'd done with her time.

Or more to the point, her name.

No carousing. No scandals. Nothing that could be considered a stain.

She'd even agreed to marry a man she thought of as her own, personal brick wall—though far less warm and approachable than any slab of stone—on her eighteenth birthday.

Well. *Agreed* was a strong word.

Randall Grant, the sixth Earl of Langston, had been her father's choice for her since she was in the cradle. Her agreement, such as it was, had never been in doubt.

Dal, as Randall was known to friends and family and the girl he'd been given, had produced the Langston family ring and handed it to her with a few cold words about the joining of their families. Because that was all that mattered.

Not Sophie herself. Not her feelings.

Certainly not love, which Sophie thought no one in either her family or Dal's had believed was real or of any import for at least the last few centuries.

And her reaction—her attempt at defiance—in the face of the life that had been presented to her as a fait accompli had comprised of a single deep breath, which Sophie had held for just a moment longer than she should have as Dal stood there, holding the ring before her.

Just a moment, while she'd imagined what might happen if she refused him—

But that was the thing. She couldn't imagine it.

Even thinking about defying her parents and all the plans they'd made for her had made her feel light-headed.

So she had said yes, as if Dal had asked her a question.

As if there had ever been any doubt.

She'd locked the heirloom ring away in her father's safe, murmuring about how she didn't dare flash it about until she was Dal's countess.

All she'd asked for was a long engagement, so she could pretend to have what passed for a normal life for just a little while—

But she hadn't. She hadn't dared. She'd only been marking what time she had left.

Until Renzo.

CHAPTER TWO

"DO IT," RENZO GROWLED, snapping Sophie back to her current peril. The dark lane. The powerful man who still held her before him, that hand on her chin. "Tell me another lie to my face. See what happens."

Sophie didn't know how to respond to him. She didn't know how to respond at all. She'd been so certain that his text had been a threat. That he had planned to come here and...do something.

To her.

Did you truly believe it was a threat? asked a small voice inside of her that sounded far too much like her mother. *Or did you imagine that Renzo might save you?*

But that was the trouble, wasn't it? No one could save her.

No one had ever been able to save her.

Sophie tried to pull her chin from his grip, but he didn't let go. And for some reason, that was what got to her. One more man was standing before her, making her do things she didn't want to do. Like the others, Renzo wasn't forcing her into anything. He wasn't brutish or horrible.

He was simply, quietly, unyieldingly exerting his will.

And Sophie was tired of bending, suddenly. She was tired of accepting what was handed to her and making the best of it when she'd never wanted it in the first place.

She'd made her own mistakes. Now she'd figure out how to live with them.

"Why did you come?" she demanded of Renzo then. "I doubt I'm the only woman you've ever spent a night with. Do you chase them all down?"

A flash of white teeth against the night. "Never. But then again, they do not typically furnish me with false names."

"How can you possibly know that if you never seek them out again?"

The look in his eyes changed. Oh, there was still that heat. That simmering temper. But now, suddenly, there was a different kind of awareness.

As if she had challenged him.

She supposed she had.

"I can think of only one reason a woman would wish to meet me the night before her wedding to another man," Renzo said then, his tone cold enough to do her father proud. But his gaze was pure fire. "Is that who you imagine I am? A gigolo on call? You merely lift a finger and here I am, willing and able to attend to your every desire?"

This time when she tipped her head back he released her chin.

"You're here, aren't you?"

"Indeed I am," Renzo said, something blistering and lethal in his voice then. "And never let it be said that I do not know my place."

"I don't know what—"

"I should have known that I was mixing with someone far above my station." His voice was scathing. The look on his face was far worse than a blow could have been, she was certain. "It is no more than we peasants are good for, is it not?"

Sophie's heart kicked so hard she was afraid it might crack a rib. "I have no idea what you're talking about."

"But of course you do. You are so blue-blooded I am surprised you do not drip sapphires wherever you walk. Is that not what you summoned me here to make clear?" He looked around again, as if he could see over the hill to the grand house that had commanded the earldom for centuries. As if he could see her family's own estates to the north. As if he knew every shameful, snobbish thing her parents had said to her over the years. "After all, what am I to you? The bastard son of a Sicilian village woman who raised me on her own, with nothing but shame and censure to ease her path. Oh, yes. And the rich men's washing, which she counted herself lucky to have."

"You don't know anything about me—" she started, determined to defend herself when the truth was, she had no defense for what she'd done. She still couldn't believe she'd actually done it.

"I knew you were a virgin, Sophie," he cut in. She still wasn't used to it, the dark and delicious way he said her name. As if it was a caress, when she remembered his caresses too well. A mirthless smile moved over his sensual mouth, but it failed to make him any less appealing. She doubted anything could. "I suppose I have no one to blame but myself for imagining that also made you an innocent."

"I don't know what you want from me."

"Another lie." Renzo let out a small, hard laugh that was about as amused as that smile. "You know exactly what I want from you."

"Then I'm glad we've had the opportunity to have this conversation at last," Sophie said, somehow managing to sound cool despite the clambering inside of her. "I apologize for not having it with you that night."

"Because you were too busy sneaking off, your tail between your legs, back to your earl and your engagement and your pretty little life in a high-class cage. Is that not so?"

It was such an apt description of Sophie's furtive behavior that morning after in Monaco—filled with the terrible mix of sick shame at her actions and something proud and defiant deep inside of her that simply refused to hate the greatest night of her life, no matter what it made her—that she had to pause for a minute. She had to try to catch her breath.

And when she did, she reminded herself that it didn't matter what he called her or what he thought about her, as painful as it might be to hear. There was a far more important issue to address.

"Renzo," she began, because it didn't matter

how little she wanted to tell him what he needed to know. It didn't matter that a single sentence would change both of their lives forever.

Their lives were already altered forever. He just didn't know it yet.

But he didn't look the slightest bit inclined to listen to her.

"What I cannot understand," he seethed at her in that same dark, dangerous way that made the night seem very nearly transparent beside him, "is why you thought you could do nothing more than click your fingers and I would come running."

"I don't know," she said quietly, something she wasn't sure she recognized stampeding through her, like fear. But much more acrid. "But here you are."

Sophie only realized she'd backed away from him when she felt the car behind her. She reached out, flattening her hands against the car's bonnet, sleek and low, a great deal like the only other vehicle she'd seen this man drive.

The stars had come out far above, but she didn't need the light they threw to illuminate the man before her. He would be burned deep into her flesh forever. She saw him when she closed her eyes. He haunted her dreams. The fact that he was standing here before her now, and no matter that he seemed to hate her, was almost too much for her to take in.

She had spent far too much time staring at pictures of him on the internet in the interim, like a lovesick teen girl, but she still remembered him from that night in Monte Carlo. She had walked away from the table of her friends, all gathered together to celebrate her upcoming nuptials at what Poppy had called her *proper hen do*. She had needed the air. A moment to catch her breath, and to stop pretending that marrying Randall filled her with joy. Or filled her with anything at all beyond the same, low-grade dread with which she'd faced every one of her familial obligations thus far.

The good news was, once she provided Dal with the requisite heir and spare, she could look forward to a happy, solitary life of charity and good works. They could live apart, only coming together at certain events annually. Or they could work together as if the family name was a brand and the two of them its ambassadors, just like her own parents.

No one would call her parents unhappy, she'd told herself as she'd tried to find her equanimity again.

But then again, no one was likely to call them happy, either.

Sophie just needed to resign herself to what waited for her. She knew that. She didn't understand why the closer she got to her wedding, the less resigned she felt.

But then she'd looked up, and there he'd been.

Renzo had been dressed in a dark suit, open at the neck, that seemed to do nothing but emphasize the long, sculpted ranginess of a body she knew at a glance was athletic in every sense of the term. His hair was a rich, too-long, dark brown, threaded through with gold, that called to mind the sorts of endless summers in the glorious sun that she had never experienced. He had the face of a poet, a sensual mouth below high cheekbones, and glorious eyes of dark, carnal amber—but he moved like a king.

She had known that he was coming for her from the first glance.

And when she lay awake at night and cataloged her sins, she knew that was the worst one. Because she hadn't turned around or headed back to her friends. She hadn't kept going, pushing her way through the crowd until she could hide herself in a bathroom somewhere. She hadn't assumed her usual mask of careless indifference that the papers she tried her best not to appear in liked to call *haughty*.

Sophie had seen temptation on a collision course with her and she'd…done absolutely nothing to avoid it.

She had stood where she was, rooted to the floor, and while she would never admit this out loud—and especially not to him—the truth was that she hadn't thought she *could* move.

One look at Renzo from across the crowded floor, right there in the grand casino, and her knees had threatened to give out.

And it didn't help, here on a forgotten country lane back home in England, that she knew precisely what he was capable of. She knew that none of her oversize, almost-farcically innocent daydreams were off the mark.

She hadn't been ready for a man of Renzo's skill, much less his uninhibited imagination.

But Sophie had always been a quick learner.

"Why am I here?" Renzo growled again.

He moved closer to her, that same erotic threat a kind of loose promise that hovered in his bones. She could see it all over his face. Worse, she could feel it echo deep within, a kind of fist in her gut and below, nothing but that same bright fire that had already destroyed her.

"There are consequences to actions," she said carefully, mimicking something her father might say, because she didn't know another way into the subject. "Surely you know that."

"Is this where the threat comes in?" Renzo's laugh was low. And not kind. "You people are all the same. Carrot and stick until you get your way. And you always get your way, don't you, Sophie?"

He was much too close then. Sophie expected him to stop, because she had nowhere to go, backed up into his car the way she was—but he didn't stop.

He kept coming.

And he didn't stop until he'd insinuated himself between her legs and bent her backward so for all intents and purposes, they were sprawled out together over the front of his car.

He was over her but not on her. If she strained

to keep her legs apart, he wasn't even touching her. And yet he might as well have scooped her up in his fists and held her fast.

"Let me up," she whispered fiercely.

Desperately.

But if Renzo heard her, he gave no sign.

He didn't claim her mouth in a bruising kiss, as she half expected, the way he had when he'd helped her from the car that night in Monaco. He held himself above her, sprawled over her body to keep her exactly where she was. Pinning her there. If she tried to move, she would be the one to rub her body against his.

And if she did...would she stop? She shuddered at the notion.

"Tell me about these consequences, *cara*," he murmured. "Tell me how you have suffered. Tell me how brave you have been to forge ahead in your gilded, pampered circumstances, feted and celebrated wherever you go, so soon to be the countess of all you survey."

His mouth was at her ear, then down along her neck, and she could feel the heat of him everywhere—but he still wasn't touching her.

Not the way she wanted him to.

And he wasn't done. "Where does your earl imagine you are tonight? Locked away in your virginal bridal suite, perhaps? Dressed in flowing white already, the living, lovely picture of the innocence he purchased?"

It was one thing for Sophie to think of herself as chattel in the privacy of her own head. It was something else entirely to hear Renzo say it, sardonic and mocking.

"He has not purchased me. I'm not a cow."

"Nor are you the virgin he expects."

"I would be shocked if he has any expectations at all."

"When marriage is commerce, *cara*, the contract is signed and sealed in the marital bed. Shall I tell you how?"

A wave of misery threated to take her over then. Sophie fought it back as best she could. "Not everyone is as…elemental as you are."

"Will you tell him why?" Renzo asked, unsmiling and much too close. "When he comes to claim his bride, will you tell him who else has been between the pale thighs he imagined were his alone to part?"

He shifted his position above her and she sucked

in a breath in a messy combination of anticipation and desire, but he only went down on one elbow so he could get his face that much closer to hers.

It made everything that much worse.

Or better, something in her whispered.

"You're disgusting," she told him. "And he won't notice either way."

"I think you underestimate your groom considerably," Renzo murmured. "What purpose is there in being an earl in the first place if not to plant a flag in unclaimed land and call it his?"

Her breath deserted her at that. "I'm not… There's no *flag*—"

But Renzo kept right on. "Why did you bother to remain pure and untouched for so long, if not to gift it to this betrothed of yours who you clearly hold in such high esteem?"

Sophie pressed her fingers hard against the metal of the car beneath her. She tried to pretend she didn't feel that instant wave of shame—but she did. Did it matter how distantly Dal treated her? She'd made a promise and she'd broken it.

Spectacularly.

Over and over again.

And then it had gotten even worse.

"I wanted to wait," she said quietly, fighting to stay calm. Or at least sound calm. "Until I didn't."

"I'm sure that distinction will please him greatly." Renzo's mouth was a scant centimeter from the sweep of her neck and she was sure—*she was sure*—that he could taste her rapid, revealing pulse. "Make sure your confession is vivid. Paint a picture. A man likes to know how many times his woman cries out another man's name and begs him not to stop."

She shoved at him then, no longer caring if that meant she was forced to touch him. She ignored the feel of his broad, sculpted shoulders beneath her palms and focused on all the emotions swirling around inside her, much too close to the surface.

But it didn't matter what she did, because Renzo was immovable. Another brick wall—except there was nothing cold about him. Nothing the least bit reserved. He *blazed* at her and she could feel it as if it was his hand between her legs, breaching her softness and pushing deep inside—

Her breath was ragged. Desperate. "My marriage is none of your business!"

She had the confused sense that she'd walked

directly into a trap. Renzo tensed, coiled tight as if he planned to spring at her.

"And yet here I am, right in the middle of it. Where you put me, Sophie. Against my will."

She shoved at him again and again, he didn't move. At all.

"If I put you there then I'll remove you. Consider yourself ejected. With prejudice."

"Why did you order me to meet you?" he asked, and though his voice was deceptively mild, his dark amber eyes gleamed in the dark and made her think of lions. Tigers. Big cats that had no place roaming about the staid English countryside. "Surely you must know you've made a grievous tactical error, *cara*. You've given me the upper hand."

"The upper hand?"

And she recognized that look on his face then. It was pure triumph, and it should have made her blood chill.

But he'd melted her in Monaco and she couldn't seem to get her preferred veneer of ice back, no matter what. Not around him.

"I know who you are," he told her with a certain relish that washed over her like a caress and then hit her in the gut. Hard. "And I have information I must assume your earl would no doubt prefer was not in the peasant hands of a bastard Sicilian."

"...information?"

But Sophie already knew what he would say. And still, there was a vanishingly small part of her that hoped against hope that he was the man she'd imagined he was—

"Exactly what his fiancée got up to one fine night in Monaco, for example," Renzo said, smashing any hopes she might have had. Of his better nature. Of what she needed to do here. Of this entire situation that seemed a bigger mistake with every passing moment. "What do you imagine he would pay to keep your indiscretions quiet? Because I already know the tabloids would throw money at me. I could name any sum I wish and humiliate two of the finest families in England with one sleazy little article. I must tell you, *cara*, I feel drunk with power."

"You..." She could hardly speak. Her worst nightmare kept getting worse and she had no idea how to stop it. Or contain it. Or even get her head around it. "You are—"

"Careful," he growled. "I would advise you not to call me names. You may find that I am far worse than any insults you throw at me."

He pushed himself back, up and off the car and away from her body. Sophie stayed where he'd left her, uncertain what to do next. She was shaking. There was water making her eyes feel too full and too glassy. And worst of all, there was that part of her that wanted him to come back and cover her again.

She was sick. That was the only explanation.

"What I am is mercenary," Renzo told her. He watched her pitilessly as she struggled to sit up. "You know what that word means, I presume?"

"Of course I know what it means." She sat for a moment, more winded than she should have been, and then pushed herself off the car to get her feet back on the ground.

But it didn't make her feel better. Maybe nothing ever would again.

"What it means to you is something derogatory, I am sure," Renzo said, still watching her in that cold, very nearly cruel way. "Everything is mercenary to those who do not need to make their own money."

Sophie understood that was a slap. "I don't—"

He merely lifted a brow and she fell silent, then hated herself for her easy acquiescence.

"Everything I have, everything I am, I created out of nothing," he told her. "I have nothing polite to say about the man who left my mother pregnant to fend for herself. I have only become a better man than he could ever dream of being. And do you know how I did that?"

"Of course I know. You raced cars for years."

"What I did, Sophie, was take every opportunity that presented itself to me. Why should this be any different?" He watched her as she straightened from the car and took a shaky step. "What consequences would you like to speak to me about?"

And she understood then.

She understood her own, treacherous heart, and why it had pushed her out here in the middle of the night to further complicate the situation she had already made untenable with what she'd done. She understood that no matter what she might have told herself about threatening texts and potential blackmail, what she'd wanted was that man she'd made up in her head in Monaco.

The man who had looked at her through a crowd

and seen her. Only her. Not her family name or her father's wealth—just her.

The man who had taken her, again and again.

The man who had learned every inch of her in the most naked, carnal, astounding way possible, there in that villa high in the hills with the glittering lights of the city so far below.

The man who had made her laugh, scream, cry, and beg him to do it all over again.

But that had just been a night. Just one night.

And he was just a man, after all. Not the savior she'd made up in her head. Not the answer to a prayer she hadn't known she'd made.

She should never, ever have answered his text. Because this had only made everything worse.

Her hand crept over her belly, because she couldn't seem to help herself.

"I thought..." she started, then stopped herself, blinking back the emotions she desperately wanted to conceal from him. "I wanted..."

"Your cake and to eat it, too. Yes? I'm familiar with the phrase." The curve of his lips was like a razor. "Why give up the bastard for the earl if you can have them both?"

"That wasn't what I wanted at all."

"Of course it was." The razor curl to his lips

edged over into outright disgust. "Do you think I don't know your type, Sophie? Cheating fiancées turn into lying wives in the blink of an eye. And bored housewives are all the same, whether their house is a hovel or a grand hall. Trust me when I tell you that Europe is littered with the detritus of broken vows. You are not as special as you might imagine."

She shook at that ruthless character assassination, but the worst part was that she couldn't manage to shove out a single word in her own defense. Of course he believed these things of her. Had she showed him anything different?

What had seemed like sunlight and glory to her had been nothing but tawdry. She had her little accident to prove it. All she had to do was imagine trying to explain her behavior to her fiancé—or worse, her father. She knew the words they would use.

And she would deserve them.

"Renzo," she said, very carefully, lest she jog something inside and send all these terrible, unwieldy things spilling out into the dirt between them. "There's something you need to know."

"I know everything I need to know." His words were terse. His judgment rendered. It only surprised her that she'd imagined he might be different. "What I cannot forgive is that you made me an unwitting part of your dishonesty. A vow means something to me, Sophie, and you made me break one."

She smiled, though it felt brittle. "What vows did you break?"

"I made a promise to myself many years ago that I would never, ever take something that belonged to another," he told her with a kind of arrogant outrage, as if she'd twisted his arm.

"You're right," she said then, because something broke inside of her. She hugged herself as she stepped back, away from him and his car and all these messy emotions she should have been smart enough to leave behind her in Monte Carlo. "I should never have come here tonight."

"These are games children play, Sophie," he told her, fury and condemnation and all that righteousness making his accent more pronounced.

"You're the one making threats," she pointed out.

"You can consider it a courtesy. One you did not extend to me when you decided to entangle me in your sick, sad little marital games."

She could do nothing but nod her head, everything within her swollen painfully and near to bursting—but she couldn't let herself give in. She couldn't show him more of herself. She couldn't allow him to hurt her any more than he already had.

Because the truth was, she didn't think she could survive it. She had been frozen solid all her life. Renzo had melted her, it was true, but Sophie hadn't understood until tonight that the ice had been her armor.

"Marry your earl or do not," Renzo said with dark finality. "But leave me out of it. Or I will assume you are inviting me to share the details of our night in Monaco with the world."

She swallowed, which was hard to do when she felt as if the tears she refused to shed were choking her. "I understand."

He didn't say another word. He stalked around to the driver's side and climbed into the car with a grace that should not have been possible for a man his size.

And Sophie stood where she was for a long time after he'd gone, driving off with a muscular roar.

She wanted to cry, but didn't allow herself the weakness.

He'd treated her like a naughty child but the truth was, Sophie thought she'd just grown up.

At last.

She already hated herself, so what was a little more fuel to that fire? She would marry Dal tomorrow, as planned. She would carry on with the life that had been so carefully plotted out for her. She would force herself to do her wifely duty and Dal would either do the math or he wouldn't.

Babies were born early all the time.

Her stomach heaved at that, but Sophie shoved the bile back down.

She'd made her bed and now she would have to lie in it. Literally.

Something in her eased at that. There was a freedom in having no good choices, she supposed. If Dal found out, it wasn't as if it would turn a good marriage bad. Their marriage was a business affair, cold and cruel at its best.

If she was lucky, he might even set her free.

That would have to be enough.

The child she carried might not be Dal's. It

might never know its real father. But no matter what, no matter what happened, it would be hers.

Hers.

And Sophie vowed she would love her baby enough, with all that she had, so that it would never know the difference.

CHAPTER THREE

RENZO WOKE IN the middle of the night, restless and something like agitated—when he normally slept like the dead.

He had left Sophie behind without a backward glance, roaring off in a cloud of self-righteousness and sweet revenge, delivered exactly as planned. He'd congratulated himself on the entire situation, and the way he'd handled it, all the way back to the suite of rooms he maintained in his Southwark hotel, with its views of the Thames and giddy, crowded London sprawled at his feet.

He would normally top off a satisfying and victorious day with enough strong drink to make him merry and an uninhibited woman to take the edges off. But, unaccountably, he had done neither of those things.

Not because he was *mourning* anything, he'd assured himself. It was nothing to him if a one-night stand who'd lied to him repeatedly was getting married. It was entirely possible every one-night stand he'd ever enjoyed had raced off to marry someone else—why should he care?

He'd sat there in the fine bar on a high floor in his hotel, surrounded by gleaming, beautiful people, none of whom likely knew the first thing about Sophie Carmichael-Jones and her wedding plans, and told himself that he felt nothing at all.

Nothing save triumph, that was.

He had been less able to lie to himself, however, when every image in his head as he'd drifted off to sleep was of Sophie and all the ways he'd had her in Monaco, each more addictive than the last. And a thousand new ways he could avail himself of her lush, remarkably acrobatic loveliness, if she'd been in the vicinity instead of off in a stately house in Hampshire, ready to wed a bloody earl in the morning.

She was a hunger that nothing else could possibly satisfy, and the fact that was so infuriated Renzo.

Still, he had been certain that come the dawn—and with it the inevitability of her high-society wedding, with all its trappings and titles and trumpeting self-regard on the pages of every tabloid rag in Europe—the raging hunger would disappear, to be replaced by his usual indifference toward anything and everything that appeared in his rearview mirror.

But here he was. Wide-awake before dawn.

His body was hot and tight and too many sensations swirled all over him, as if Sophie was beside him in this bed when he knew very well she was not.

He rolled out of the wide platform bed and refused to handle his body's demands on his own. His lips thinned at the thought.

Renzo was not an adolescent boy, all testosterone and infatuation. He would not use his own hands and spill his own seed with the name of an unattainable female on his lips, as if he was fifteen. He hadn't done such things when he'd actually been fifteen, for that matter, loping around the ancient cliffside town where he'd been the no-account bastard son of a shamed whore of a mother—and therefore might as well have been invisible to the village girls.

He wasn't invisible now. The village girls who had snubbed him then were grown now. Married to the men they'd found more appropriate and settled there on the edge of the very cliff that Renzo had imagined throwing himself over, more than once, to escape the realities of a bastard's life in that place. And these days Renzo's illegitimacy was rarely mentioned. He was the local celebrity who had not only gone on to a glorious motor racing career, but had systematically bought and rebuilt every structure in that damned town, then opened a hotel on the next ridge, until there was no doubt in anyone's mind who the king of that tiny little village was.

That was how Renzo handled things. He waited. He bought it.

Then he made it his.

But that wasn't possible in this situation. He padded over to the wall of windows that let in the insistent gleam of one of the world's premiere cities, but he didn't see London Bridge there before him. Or the Shard.

It was as if Sophie was haunting him, though Renzo had never before believed in ghosts.

There, alone in the dark with only London as witness, he no longer felt that sense of triumph.

Instead, he remembered her responses. The catch in her throat. The wonder in her gaze.

The way she'd looped her arms around his neck when he'd lifted her against the wall—directly inside the front door to his villa, because he couldn't wait another moment—and had blushed.

From head to toe, as he'd soon discovered.

He had quickly learned that she was a virgin, and he'd reveled in that fact. That she was entirely his. That he was the only man alive to taste her, touch her, learn how she delighted in every new thing he taught her.

Renzo had never been a possessive man. But Sophie had brought it out in him.

Earlier tonight he'd accused her of being a virgin as a technicality only.

He wanted to believe that, of course. A woman who was meant to be a countess might well keep her hymen intact in preparation for her marriage while involving herself in all manner of other debaucheries. He'd met women like that before—hell, he'd happily participated in the debauchery.

He'd wanted nothing more than to make Sophie pay for thinking that she could pull one over on him. Or perhaps what he had really wanted to make her pay for was the fact that she'd succeeded.

But the truth was, he realized as he stood there and stared out at a city he completely failed to see, it didn't make sense.

Renzo knew any number of mercenary women. They were a lot like him, each and every one of them. They knew what they wanted and they proceeded to go out there and get it. They used everything they had. Status if they had it. Wiles if they did not. Whatever it took to get what they wanted.

He had learned to recognize one of his ilk from afar. Long before they made it into his bed, Renzo knew them for that steel in their gaze and their particular brand of avid keenness. He had never been wrong.

And he'd never been caught by a grifter like himself, either.

Renzo might have convinced himself otherwise since he'd received that newspaper clipping by post, but he hadn't read that kind of sharpness in Sophie.

Not when she'd been calling herself Elizabeth, flowing like sweet honey all over his hands, and charming him within an inch of his life.

Renzo was not easily charmed.

It occurred to him then—high over the Thames

in the middle of the night with nothing in his head but the only woman who had ever deceived him—that it was possible he had been hasty.

He had been so busy scoring points, making sure he got in as many digs at her as possible, that he hadn't allowed himself to really listen to the things she said.

And more, the things she hadn't said.

He, of all people, should have known better. After all, he'd spent his entire childhood trying to live up to the fantasy of what he'd imagined he ought to have been and what becoming it would do for him. If he was perfectly well behaved. If he transcended the poverty in which he'd been raised. If he never, ever, allowed what others thought of him or his circumstances to hold him back. If he made his own way in the world, as best he could, whatever that looked like. If he made himself a star in his chosen field and instead of throwing his money away like so many of his peers, used it to build himself a little empire.

If he did all the right things, he'd told himself for far longer than he should have, surely that would gain his father's notice.

But it never had.

Not in the way he wanted, anyway. And when he'd decided to force the issue, it hadn't ended well.

Renzo's idealism, immature and pathetic by any estimation, had been fully beaten out of him in his eighteenth year, courtesy of the very wealthy, very titled prince who had left his mother pregnant with him. Literally beaten it out of him. He'd had relapses since then, it was true, but he'd always learned the same damned lesson in the end.

Meeting his father had taught Renzo that there were no better places or people, as he'd been tempted to imagine. There were no misunderstandings that explained away eighteen years of poverty and shame. There was only reality and in it, people did what suited them with little or no thought to the effect that their actions might have on others.

If it was impossible to conceive of how a person could do something heinous to someone else, a good rule of thumb was to assume that person had been thinking only and ever of themselves.

That lesson had been pounded into Renzo's fool head again and again and again, particularly during that one vile week when he'd been eighteen and stupid and had foolishly imagined his own father would treat him well because of their blood tie. He knew better now.

Still, he'd let this woman throw him.

He knew all about women like Sophie Carmichael-Jones. They thought themselves so high-and-mighty, so far above the peasants—but at the end of the day, they were motivated by money. The same as Renzo's mother had been, desperate to keep a roof over her head by any means possible. The same as Renzo had learned to be, making certain he excelled at whatever he did to pay her bills. The only difference was that the Carmichael-Joneses of the world believed their own scrabbling for cash was more meaningful, somehow, because it was wrapped up in estates and titles, ancient claims and other such things.

Renzo did not share this belief.

A hustler was a hustler, in his estimation.

He couldn't believe he hadn't seen the signs in Sophie, his sad-eyed innocent with the prettiest smile he'd ever beheld.

She'd spoken to him of consequences and he'd thought he'd give her a few—but hours later, he couldn't seem to get that particular word out of his head.

He crossed his arms over his chest and found himself scowling down at the Thames as it wound on, unheeding, the same as it had done for centuries.

It had taken more self-control than he'd imagined it would to be near Sophie again and not take her.

His body had reacted as if they had been lovers for decades. He had been hard and ready the instant he'd seen her come out of the shadows. Even then, when he knew who she really was and had no intention whatsoever of giving her access to him again, his body had made its own wishes known.

He wanted her despite everything. Still. Now.

He hadn't known, from one moment to the next, which one of them he was more furious at. Her, for the lies she had told him and the way she'd made him complicit in her own betrayal of her fiancé. Or him, for wanting her with an edge that bordered on desperation, even then.

Consequences, something in him whispered.

He remembered how she'd stood there before him in the close, wet dark.

Gone was the glowing, carefree woman who'd given herself to him so freely in Monaco. In England, apparently, Sophie was drawn. Agitated.

And had kept holding a hand over her belly, as if her meal had not quite agreed with her…

Consequences, he thought again.

And found himself cursing in a fluid, filthy Sicilian dialect when another possibility altogether occurred to him.

He'd believed he was furious before.

But now…

Renzo thought a far better word to describe his feelings was *volcanic.*

Sophie woke in a confused, hurtling rush and her first thought was that it was much too early to be awake. The light was thin and halting, creeping in between the curtains she'd neglected to close as if uncertain of its reception.

Her second thought was that today was her wedding day.

And that unpleasant reality slapped at her, waking her up even more whether she liked it or not.

"I can see you are not asleep," came a familiar voice from much too close. "It is best to stop pretending, Sophie."

It was voice that should not have been anywhere near her, not here.

Not in Langston House where, in a few short hours, she would become the latest in a long line of unenthused countesses.

She told herself she was dreaming even though her eyes were wide-open.

Sophie took her time turning over in her bed, then sitting up gingerly as if she expected it to hurt, somehow. And still, no matter how long she stared or blinked, she couldn't make Renzo disappear.

He lounged there at the foot of the four-poster bed, here in her bedroom in Langston House as if she'd conjured him up from one of the dreams that had plagued her all night.

"What are you doing here?" she asked, her voice barely more than a whisper.

"It turns out we have more to discuss."

She didn't like the way he said that, dark and something like lethal.

"How did you get in here?" Sophie looked

around wildly. She didn't know what she expected to find. Her father bursting through the door, perhaps, assuming Renzo had barged his way into Langston House like some kind of marauder? Or even Poppy, always so concerned, calling out her name?

But it really was early. If she ignored the wild pounding in her chest, there was no sound. Anywhere. No one seemed to be awake but the two of them. Langston House felt still all around.

And Renzo was *here*.

Right *here*, in this bedroom Sophie had been installed in as the future Countess of Langston. It was all tapestries, priceless art, and frothy antique chairs that looked too fragile to sit in, as befitted a room that regularly appeared in guidebooks.

"You can't be here," she managed to say, clutching the bedclothes to her like some kind of security blanket.

"Talk to me some more about the consequences you mentioned, if you please," Renzo said mildly. So mildly it made every hair on her body seem to stand straight up in warning.

He was dressed the way he had been the night before. Dark trousers and boots, sleek and spare, as if to highlight his lean, brooding athleticism. That thick hair of his looked messy, as if he'd spent the hours since she'd last seen him running his fingers through it again and again. The leather jacket he'd worn in the rain last night was open now over the kind of soft, impossibly simple T-shirt that looked as if it was nothing more than a throwaway piece—and yet clung to his sculpted chest, hugging him and exalting him in turn, and likely costing more than some people's mortgages.

If she was a better person, Sophie thought, she wouldn't find him so attractive, even now, when she knew exactly what kind of trouble he'd brought into her life. When she knew that she should have walked away from him that night in Monte Carlo and let him remain nothing but a daydream she might have taken out and sighed over throughout the coming years of her dry, dutiful marriage.

It took a moment for his words to penetrate. And when they did, a kind of icicle formed inside of her, sharp and long and frigid.

"I don't know what you mean," she said, her lips too dry and her throat not much better.

"I think you do." Renzo stood at the foot of her

bed, one hand looped around one of the posts in a lazy, easy sort of grip that did absolutely nothing to calm Sophie's nerves. Not when she was sure she could feel that same hard, steady hand wrapped around her neck. Or much, much lower.

"I think you came to tell me something last night but let my temper scare you off. Or perhaps it would be more accurate to say you used my temper as an excuse to keep from telling me, would it not?"

Sophie found her hands covering her belly again, there beneath her comforter. Worse, Renzo's dark gaze followed the movement, as if he could see straight through the pile of soft linen to the truth.

"What would be accurate to say is that you took the opportunity last night to make an uncomfortable situation worse," she said, sounding more in control than she felt. She very deliberately removed her hands from her belly and set them on the top of her blankets where Renzo could see them. Where they could be inoffensive and tell him nothing. "That's on you. It has nothing at all to do with me."

"It has everything to do with you, *cara*."

"I would like you to leave," she told him, fighting to keep her voice calm. "You've threatened me already. I don't know what showing up here, hours before I'm meant to marry, could possibly accomplish. Or is this more punishment?"

Renzo's lips quirked into something no sane person would call a smile. He didn't move and yet he seemed to loom there, growing larger by the second and consuming all the air in the bedchamber.

He made it hard to breathe. Or see straight.

Or remember why, exactly, she'd marched back up to Langston House last night filled with new resolve about what she would do and how she would manage her marriage—no matter Dal's reaction to her pregnancy. Assuming she even told him.

She was aware that such concerns made her a terrible person. On some level, she thought she would always hate herself for the things she'd found herself thinking in these awful days. But none of that mattered.

What mattered was keeping her baby safe, one way or another. She couldn't afford to care too much what that looked like.

"We will get to punishments in a moment," Renzo said. His dark amber gaze raked over her, bold and harsh. His sensual mouth, the one she'd felt on every inch of her skin and woke in the night yearning for again, flattened. "First, answer me one question, and do not lie to me. Do not imagine for one millisecond that I will not know if you do, because believe me, I will. And a lie will only make this worse for you."

"That is very hard to imagine."

But he didn't respond to that. His gaze bored into her, so hard and deep she was sure he left marks. "Are you with child, Sophie?"

CHAPTER FOUR

SOPHIE SUCKED IN a shocked, harsh breath that she was instantly afraid announced her guilt in no uncertain terms.

The way Renzo's mouth twisted at the sound, she thought it had.

Her heart was pounding so loud and wild that she was astonished it didn't knock her backward. She sat up straighter as if that could keep such a thing from happening, her throat tight with fear and every muscle in her body tense.

She hadn't slept enough, too busy tossing and turning and looking for solutions to her problem that didn't involve any more deception—or any loveless marriages, for that matter. Her head was too fuzzy as a result and she knew that that was nothing but a liability where Renzo was concerned. He was like a steamroller, for all that he was so beautiful, and the real problem was that there was a small part of her that wanted to make it easy for him.

It was more than a small part of her, if she was honest. All it wanted was to simply lie back, surrender, and let him do with her what he would.

But she reminded herself why he was here. Why she even knew him.

Sophie had stepped out of line exactly once. She'd sneaked out of her cage, thrown caution to the wind, and this was the result.

She'd handed over her innocence to a man who could not possibly understand what it was she'd surrendered to him. And then she'd allowed herself to imagine, like some kind of child, that he could rescue her from this life she'd been born into. That she could see him again the night before her wedding and feel that same sense of impossible homecoming she'd felt in his villa in Monaco. That he would somehow make it all okay.

But he wasn't that man. *That man doesn't exist*, she told herself harshly.

And if last night had taught her anything, it was that throwing away her safe, knowable, perfectly plotted-out life for a taste of passion led to nothing but being left there on the side of a country lane. In the rain.

Pregnant on the side of the road, literally.

Sophie knew she had nobody to blame for that but herself.

"I think that you are carrying a child," Renzo was saying, low and furious, that lazy grip of his on the post…harder. Tighter. "*My* child. And you must understand that if that is so, I cannot permit you to go ahead with this wedding of yours."

"It's not up to you," she managed to say. "Think of all the things you called me last night. What makes you imagine that I would obey you in anything?"

"I have so far been very kind to you, *cara*. I would advise you not test the boundaries of my patience."

"I didn't send you that newspaper clipping." Sophie sat straighter, even though it made her spine ache. "I didn't summon you here. I thought you texted me…" She shook her head. "Why would anyone do such a thing? I assumed it was a threat. And, sure enough, when you appeared, you set about threatening me as soon as possible."

"Did you feel threatened?" Renzo asked softly,

that edge in his voice much worse than anything he'd said. "Let me assure you, Sophie, that I have not begun to threaten you. Last night was a game. This, here, this lie you tell with every breath…" He shook his head, though his gaze never left her. "I am no longer playing."

"I think you have me confused with someone who cares whether you are playing games or not," Sophie told him, with tremendous composure she was nowhere near feeling.

Renzo dropped his arm to his side and it was astonishing how much more threatening that was. As if he was no longer bothering to pretend that he was in any way at his ease—something that could only bode ill for Sophie.

"I will ask you one more time," he growled at her, his accent more pronounced, as if to indicate exactly how far south this was headed. Assuming there was a worse place to go than him here, in her bedroom at Langston House, with her and Dal's entire families and wedding parties in residence. "Are you carrying my child? Is that the consequence you dared not tell me about last night?"

Sophie wished she wasn't in bed, her hair everywhere, wearing nothing but a flimsy little sleeping gown. She wished she was wrapped in sheets of armor. Encased in steel. She tried to pretend that she was tough and strong and brave—anything but what she was, a scared twenty-six-year-old in deep over her head with this man, in a situation she'd caused.

That was the part that made her the most panicky. The fact that *she* had done this. No one had done it to her. She could so easily have stayed with her friends that night in Monte Carlo, stayed the virgin she was expected to be, and woken up in the morning prepared to meet her obligations as expected.

Without a brand-new pregnancy that should never have happened in the first place, or the sort of unfortunate connection to a Sicilian race car driver that would send her father into paroxysms of rage.

Oh, the things she wished.

Sophie told herself it didn't matter what she wished or how she felt, it only mattered what she allowed Renzo to see. And even that mattered only insofar as it allowed her to clean up her own mess.

"Here's a hypothetical." She cleared her throat,

wishing her mouth wasn't so dry. "Let's say you were, in fact, the father of a child who came about thanks to a one-night stand that should never have happened. That no one must ever suspect happened. What then? What claim do you imagine that gives you?"

"What claim?" He bared his teeth at her. "It gives me the only claim. My child, my claim."

"That might be more meaningful if I was a free woman," Sophie said quietly. "But I am not."

"That sounds a great deal like your problem, not mine. And certainly not my child's."

"You were a mistake," Sophie said, emphasizing that last word. "What right do you imagine you have to barge into my life and change it now? I never promised you anything. And I don't recall you making any pledges yourself."

"I don't think you have the slightest idea what I might have done, since you sneaked off before I woke."

She rolled her eyes. "Which you, in all your years of playing the field in the full glare of the tabloids, never did. Not even once. You preferred to lounge about and spend the mornings with each and every one of your conquests, making affirmations and discussing commitment over breakfast."

"None of them fell pregnant."

"How would you know?" she asked. "Did all the vows you exchanged after your single night in their company extend to them sharing their fertility status with you weeks later?"

"I know because I have never failed to use protection before."

"Until me," Sophie said, and couldn't quite keep her tone as mild as she would have liked. "What luck."

Renzo didn't say anything. And despite herself, Sophie remembered how it had happened. When he'd lifted her against him, right there against the wall. When he'd somehow understood—almost instantly—how little experience she had. He'd laid her down right there on the floor and had taken his time. He'd stripped her as if the act of removing her clothes was a caress.

Then he'd set his mouth between her legs and utterly destroyed her.

And after that, things had only gotten more intense.

But there was no use thinking about any of that

now. There was no point and there was certainly no use. She was as trapped as she'd ever been. His presence here didn't change that—it just made what she had to do that much worse.

"In any case," Sophie said when the silence dragged on too long, "this is not my decision to make. After our wedding, I will speak to the earl and see how he wishes to handle things."

"Know this, if nothing else. Your little earl has no authority over my child."

"But what he does have is authority over me," Sophie threw back at him with all the anguish she'd been bottling up inside of her these last weeks. "He will be my husband in a matter of hours and, as perhaps you might have guessed, it is not a modern arrangement. It will be quite traditional, and I imagine the decision—all decisions—will not be mine to make. And if that's the case, believe me, they will certainly not be yours to make, either."

She hardly knew what she was saying. She couldn't imagine Dal asserting his authority over anything—he was far too cold. Remote. He would be far more likely to curl his lip and banish her to a family parcel of land off in the Shetland

Islands or somewhere equally far enough away to feel like an appropriate prison.

But she saw no reason to share that with Renzo.

She didn't know what she expected. But it wasn't the laugh that Renzo let out then, loud and long. She might even have thought it was a real laugh if she'd never heard the other.

And if she felt a terrible pang at the thought of his real laughter, spilling over her like light and heat as they sprawled there in his wide bed in Monaco—well. Her entire life was a story of compromises she'd made even before being asked, because that was her role. Sacrifices that only seemed so in retrospect, when she realized what it was she'd missed out on. Obligation over everything, even common sense.

That was what being the Carmichael-Jones heiress meant. That was what it had always meant.

It took precedence over everything, even this. Especially this.

"I will assume that all of this is your roundabout way of telling me that yes, you are indeed pregnant," Renzo said, his voice sounding rougher than usual. Thicker, maybe. Harsher. "You were a virgin when I met you. I can therefore only assume that the baby is mine, as I suspected."

"There is a great deal of debate on that," she told him, tilting her chin up as if she thought he might take a swing at her. As if she wanted him to. "After you, I thought—why not take a tour of Europe? From one bed to the next until I got my fill. As you do. So really, it could be anyone's."

All Renzo did was shift his weight. Or move again without seeming to move at all. She thought his eyes got darker. Or they landed more heavily on her, somehow. All she knew was that the world seemed to shift, then tilt, and all she could seem to do was hold on to the bed beneath her and hope for the best.

He did not dignify her claims of sleeping her way across Europe with a response, which only made her want to provoke him all the more.

She told herself she had no earthly idea why she would do such a thing.

"You should consider your next move very carefully," Renzo told her matter-of-factly. As if he was a general delivering orders to troops whose lives depended on obeying him. "You should bear in mind that I could make a scene now. I could have half the house in this room in the next five minutes, to witness you and me in bed together, mere hours before your wedding. I'd invite you to ask yourself how you think your friends and family would handle such a thing."

Sophie could imagine it all too well. Her father would become apoplectic as his dynastic dreams faded away before his very eyes. Her mother might actually swoon from the shame of it. She even imagined that Dal might allow his expression to frost over into an expression of refined disgust, the deepest feeling she imagined he was capable of experiencing.

Beyond that, Sophie herself would be humiliated, and on a grand scale. The guests would inevitably sell their stories, which Sophie's parents would find almost more unpalatable than the story itself, and which Sophie could expect to haunt her. The wedding would be off, of course. The things that an earl might choose to ignore years into his arranged marriage and after Sophie had dutifully given him children, he would, naturally, be unable to overlook today.

A cheating wife was one thing, especially when they could expect to have little relationship of their own. Or so it seemed with all the people Sophie knew in her claustrophobic circles. But a cheating fiancée with the gall to parade her lover beneath his roof mere hours before the wedding ceremony? That was something else.

If it wasn't, Sophie's father would never have spent all these years lecturing her mercilessly on the value of virtue.

"I'm sure it would be fine," she said now, trying to brazen her way through.

Renzo did not look the least bit impressed with the attempt.

"I'm going to allow you the opportunity to do the right thing," he told her, almost kindly. But she could see his face and she knew that whatever else was motivating him right now, it wasn't *kindness.* "Let us be clear, you and I. You do not deserve this courtesy from me. It is a measure, *cara mia*, of what a forgiving man I am. Charitable unto my soul. If I were you, I would consider flinging yourself at my feet to show your gratitude."

Last night Sophie had been afraid she might cry. This morning, however, that feeling was gone. It had been replaced by this…flashing thing like lightning that swirled around inside of her and made her want nothing more than to land a punch or two. The way he kept doing.

"Charitable. Forgiving." She shook her head. "I think perhaps you're translating the words wrong from Italian, Renzo."

"Is that a dig?" His smile then was so sharp she thought it could have cut steel into tiny shavings. "Be aware, Sophie. I am not your earl. I was not raised with silver spoons stuffed in every orifice, starched and scrubbed within an inch of my life into some cordial automaton. I am not polite. I am not courteous. I was raised with nothing and was forced to make everything that I now possess. And I will do anything to keep what is mine." That smile began to remind her of nothing so much as fangs. "You have no idea what you have done. None at all."

He looked scary and intense, and there was a time—perhaps only a few hours ago—where she would have found that almost too much to bear. But he had said and done these things to her already, and here she still was. She could bear anything.

And the light coming through her heavy curtains was no longer quite so pale or insubstantial. It looked like sunlight.

Her wedding day had arrived, despite her best efforts and no matter that there had been a reappearance of the shockingly beautiful—if wildly overwhelming—Sicilian there before her.

It had been profoundly childish to imagine she could escape this particular noose around her neck. She didn't know how she'd managed to pretend, for even a moment, that she might somehow manage to buck the tremendous weight of two ancient families' expectations. No matter what she'd done.

Sophie made a big show of yawning, complete with a theatrical stretch.

"Oh, I'm so sorry," she murmured, though she kept her gaze locked to his. "Blah-blah-blah. I will pay. I will rue the day. I will cry myself to sleep and your name will be a curse." She sounded so bored she was surprised she could sit upright, and she waved a languid hand to underscore her tone. "This is all very melodramatic and the truth is, you've jumped to a lot of mad, unsubstantiated conclusions. You're lucky I haven't called to have you thrown out of this house. But I will. You have exactly five seconds to go before I do."

"Do you truly wish to test me, Sophie?" Renzo drawled, so soft and deadly it shivered over her skin like its own breeze. "Can you really believe I am a man to be trifled with? I would not have imagined you could be so foolish."

There was some kind of devil in her, needling her. Kicking at her. It made her want to open up her mouth and say something else he wouldn't be able to forgive. It made her want to hurt him, however she could—

She wanted to hurt him the way he'd hurt her last night.

Sophie felt the air go out of her at that. Was that really who she was? She wanted to hurt this man because he wasn't the fantasy she'd built in her head? Could anyone have lived up to that?

Or had she known he couldn't—that no one could?

Did you simply want justification to swan off into the prison of this marriage and get to feel superior and self-righteous? asked a little voice within.

Condemning her thoroughly with a simple question she didn't want to answer.

And as if he could see it, or simply knew it somehow in that way he seemed to know all sorts of things about her he shouldn't, Renzo smiled again.

This time she thought it might cut her in half.

"Do what you must," he told her, with a quiet sort of conviction that made it too hard, suddenly, to sit still. "Have whatever conversations you feel you need to have. I will leave you to it. And I will expect you on that very same lane where you met me last night. You have two hours."

"Or what?" she asked.

Her heart was thumping again, even louder, and so hard she felt vaguely ill. But her voice was barely a whisper.

"You don't want to know *or what*," Renzo assured her. "Trust me on this."

And with that, he turned toward the door.

Sophie couldn't understand what was happening inside of her. There was that lightning flash, urging her on to do things she knew were well-nigh suicidal. There was that reservoir of something thicker, deeper. *Sadder*, something in her whispered. The part of her that remembered him different than this. The part that remembered him generous and like sunshine.

Her brief escape, not a prison all his own.

And more than that she felt something hollow, like an ache that only kept expanding, that wanted things she couldn't seem to make sense of in her own head.

Maybe that was why she was up and on her feet without giving herself a moment to consider it. To think better of it.

But then again, had she really had a wholly coherent thought since the doctor had come back in with the news she hadn't wanted at her physical a few days ago?

Sophie had no time to consider that question now, because she scrabbled to the side of the bed and charged across the floor, chasing that long-legged stride of his. And then she threw herself at him, or close enough.

She grabbed at his arm, which didn't help anything. His leather coat was desperately soft, covering a bicep that appeared to be sculpted from stone. Renzo cast a glance down at her grip, then her face, his sensual mouth flat.

Something hectic glittered in his dark amber eyes like a warning Sophie knew she should heed.

"You can't just come in here and throw all these threats around," she hissed at him.

"I think you will find that I did exactly that," he said in that menacingly soft way of his that should have stopped her dead. And possibly made her cry, too. "Because I can. And more than that, you must understand that these are not idle threats. These are promises. If I were you, I would make peace with that now."

"What do you think is going to happen?" she threw at him, furious and panicked and something else she dared not name. "You are going to ruin my life and why? Just to hurt me? You must know that anything you do to hurt me will hurt this baby, too."

He reached down and put his hand over hers, then peeled her fingers from his arm, demonstrating his superior strength slowly and implacably and without hurting her at all.

Which, of course, made it worse.

"No child of mine will know a moment's want," Renzo told her, something dark she couldn't understand in his voice. "Ever. You, on the other hand, I will maintain only as long as necessary. Why? Do you have a list of demands?"

"I don't want to be 'maintained,'" she hurled at him, as if he'd struck a blow.

She cradled the hand he'd removed from his arm as if his fingers on her skin had left blisters.

"Do you not?" Renzo asked, his dark eyes ablaze. "What, then, do you anticipate your marriage will give you? Or is it that you prefer a certain kind of cage to call your own?"

She shook her head, and opened her mouth to refute him—but he wasn't finished.

"If the bars are pretty and look like the British aristocracy, then why not—is that it?" He was much taller than she remembered when she stood this close to him, and it reminded her that he was entirely too strong, as well. Why was she provoking him? What did she imagine she had to gain from it? "Sadly, Sophie, I'm afraid that you lay down with a dog of the first order. Now you must handle the fleas. The child you carry is a mutt. *My* mutt. And your blue blood turns muddier by the moment." He inclined his head. "You have my condolences."

"I don't understand why, if you think so little

of me, you would go to the trouble to disrupt my wedding and—"

"I do not think so little of you," he told her, stern and uncompromising, though that ferocious gleam in his dark eyes told a different story altogether. "I do not think of you at all. All you are to me is a liar who happens to carry within her the only thing I care about in this world."

Sophie felt as if she was swallowing broken glass. She felt as if she was reeling, though she didn't think she'd actually tipped over.

"That's a remarkable amount of pressure to put on child who hasn't even been born yet," she said quietly. "And I didn't sign up to be your brood mare, Renzo."

"Listen to me."

He bent down, putting his face entirely too close to hers, and it wasn't until her back came up hard against the wall behind her that she realized he had moved her all the way across the room. Then he made it worse, placing a hand flat against the wall on either side of her head.

A cage in fact. No longer only in theory.

And Sophie despaired of herself, because her reaction was…fire.

Everywhere.

Renzo leaned in closer. "I am the bastard son of a man so grand and glorious he never condescended to so much as speak my name, much less extend a hand to aid me or the woman who bore me in any way. My mother worked her fingers to the bone—which I am certain is nothing but an expression a person like you might use to be poetic. Descriptive. But when I say it, it is not figurative." Something seemed to vibrate through him, as dark and magnetic as that harsh light in his gaze.

"Her hands were cracked and bleeding. She had wounds that never healed, particularly in the winter. And still she worked. She washed clothes and mended them. She scrubbed floors. If she had pride, she cast it aside and spent eighteen years on her knees so that I might grow and prosper. And all the while, the titled, pampered pig who took his pleasure from her and then cast her aside, lived in luxury far away, where he could pretend neither she nor I existed."

Renzo was breathing hard, as if he'd just run five miles, and that should have terrified her.

Sophie had no idea why instead, all she wanted

to do was reach out and try to hold him to her, something she knew—*she knew*—he would never allow.

"This will never occur to a child of mine," he told her, and Sophie understood he wasn't simply saying it. She understood that it was a vow.

"That would never happen." There was a ringing in her head that she couldn't seem to clear, no matter how hard she tried. "I am not penniless. And neither is—"

"You misunderstand me." Renzo's voice was flat, hard. "I would not care if you were next in line to a throne, Sophie. My child will not be illegitimate. He will not only never be treated like a bastard, he will, in fact, never, ever be one."

"My child will not be a bastard," Sophie said, very deliberately. Very carefully, because she was so close she could see the play of his muscles beneath his skin, and all of it washed through her like a warning. "Because I'm getting married in a few hours."

"And even if I were inclined to allow such a thing, which I'm not, how do you imagine that will go down?" Renzo shook his head. "I cannot tell if you're truly this naive or if you're delusional. Your earl will no more take on the by-blow of his new wife's ill-considered affair than he will fly naked over the moon. The fact you imagine otherwise is troubling."

"You have obviously never met the earl. He is not an emotional man." She shrugged, as if she wasn't caged between his arms, up against the wall on the morning of her wedding. "As far as I can tell, he cares about absolutely nothing—least of all me."

"He is a man, Sophie," Renzo said, and he dipped his head, making her more aware of how close he was. "Never forget this."

How he held her there against the wall without having to put so much as a finger on her. Her hands were at her sides, her fingertips digging into the wall behind her. But she didn't know if it was because she was trying to steady herself, or desperately trying to keep her hands from touching him of their own accord.

"Your groom is a very, very wealthy man, in fact, with a lineage that I am quite certain stretches back to some damp medieval vault somewhere, stacked high with the desiccated corpses of earls just like him. He may not care about you. He may not care about anything on this earth. But here is what I can promise you." Renzo was so close then that Sophie could feel each word like a lick against her neck. "He will care, very much, if you attempt to pass off another man's child as his heir."

Her chest was rising and falling much too fast. She'd thought the urge to cry had left her, drying out forever after what had happened last night out on that deserted road, but she felt the prick of tears again. There behind her eyes, where she could neither blink them away nor control them.

"Renzo—" she began, having no idea what she could possibly say next.

But it didn't matter.

"You are still so beautiful," Renzo said, as if it hurt him. "And yet listen to you. Like all pretty things, you are rotten beneath it, aren't you?"

He murmured that almost like a poem, and somehow, that made it hurt worse. As if he'd reached deep into her, taken great handfuls of her insides and tangled them up before shoving them back haphazardly.

Making certain she would never, ever be the same again.

"I don't want any of this," she whispered.

"Do you not?" he asked, and his gaze seemed darker. Or maybe she was just afraid he could see more deeply inside of her. So deeply she was worried that he saw things she didn't even know were there. "I think you are a liar."

"Of course you do. What a shock."

"I think you lie to yourself all the time," he continued in his relentless way. "What other explanation can there be? You could have stayed right here last night and I would never have been the wiser. You didn't have to come out and speak to me, if you truly believed I was a threat to you. Once you did, you could have steered the conversation away from any hint of *consequence*. But you did not."

He reached over then and traced a faint pattern over her cheekbone, then down the line of her jaw. She felt her hands curl into fists at her side, because this felt like nothing more than a mockery of that beautiful night they had shared. When he had done exactly this, but it had all been so different. His every touch had been a reverence.

When now, it was the opposite.

She couldn't bear it, she thought. She kept thinking it.

And she kept discovering that she could bear almost anything. No matter how it tore her apart inside.

"Is that a tear, Sophie?" Renzo asked with that quiet malice that hurt her. Everywhere. And yet set her alight all the same. "I don't believe that, either."

And then he covered her mouth with his.

Which, Sophie realized in that same blazing instant, was exactly what she'd wanted.

CHAPTER FIVE

HER HEART GAVE a terrific jolt, whether in need or recognition of her own complicity she didn't know, and Sophie's hands came up.

In defense, perhaps. To ward him off or push him away, she told herself—

But all she did was find the soft fabric of his T-shirt, stretched there across his granite-hard abdomen, and then she gripped him, making fists in the material.

And surrendered to the glorious assault of his mouth on hers.His mouth was a punishment. And Sophie was sick—she had to be far sicker than she'd ever imagined possible—because she exulted in it.

It was what she'd wanted last night, out there in the wet dark. It was what she'd wanted when she'd woken up to find him there at the end of her bed.

This—he—was exactly what she wanted.

Because she ached between her legs, in that

place only he had ever found. Her breasts felt hard and heavy, as if he didn't need to touch them to make them his. She couldn't seem to help the little noises—of greed, of longing, of total surrender—that she made in the back of her throat.

Renzo made a low, rough sound that was little more than a growl, and knocked around inside of Sophie like a song. He bent, then hauled her up against him, his hands moving to take her thighs and pull her legs around his waist.

And still he kept his mouth on hers, a delicious torment. A bittersweet temptation.

All she wore was the soft, short gown she'd slept in, and Renzo acted as if it wasn't there. He kept his mouth fused to hers, and used the wall behind them to keep her where he wanted her. His trousers were a faint abrasion against the soft expanse of her inner thighs, and it was hard to find purchase against the buttery soft leather of his jacket.

She couldn't help but think of that night in his villa when he'd swung her against the wall, just like this, and had kissed her with this same mad passion—and then had slowed himself down to take her where he wanted to go, but much more carefully.

There was nothing careful about Renzo this morning.

And the only thing Sophie felt about that was a curious sense of...*elation.*

But then Renzo was reaching between them, those long, infinitely sure fingers slipping beneath the little scrap of lace she wore to find her where she was the most soft. Where she was bright and molten and entirely his, no matter what she might have tried to tell herself.

"This is the only part of you that does not lie," he said against her mouth, hard and dark.

And she wanted to protest, but his fingers moved then, parting her and playing with her.

She thrashed against him, feeling that touch of his everywhere. It was fire that grew and grew with every pass of his clever fingers, and a wild, insane need that she'd convinced herself she'd made seem more intense than it really was over these past weeks.

She discovered that if anything, she had seriously downplayed Renzo's effect on her.

"There is not a single thing that comes out of your mouth that I trust," he told her, grim and furious, but even so, the words fell through her like need. Like longing. He reached between them and she heard the sound of his zipper, but could do nothing but shudder. And yearn. "This is the only thing I trust."

She felt the broad head of him against her entrance, and then he was thrusting inside, a deep, thick, irrevocable claim. He had her pinned to the wall, caught between him and a slab of stone—and of the two of them, she thought the stone was more yielding.

Sophie cried out at his intense possession, and his mouth was on hers again.

And then everything got serious.

Scorching need. Searing and wholly mad, and she couldn't seem to care the way she knew she should.

There was only his mouth on hers, a granite, sensual tease. There was only the hardest part of him, slick and deep inside her, rocketing them both into sheer delight with every bone-rattling thrust.

She was nothing but a red-hot, greedy fist of pure sensation.

It was better than she remembered.

He was better.

And she was lost.

It was all she could do to hang on for dear life while he tested that impressive length of his again and again, slamming into her so hard and so deep it was as if he made them both new.

She began to shake. It started deep inside, then fanned out, rolling over her like a wave.

"This is the truth about you, Sophie," he told her, ferocious and cruel and yet she clung to him. She wanted him. God, how she wanted him. "You lie and you cheat and you walk around dressed to shine, blue-blooded and untouchable. But *this*. This is who you really are."

He thrust in once again, harder than before, and she ignited.

The wildfire consumed her. She shook and she clenched. She lost herself in the molten, delirious rush.

And she heard him murmur a word she didn't understand as he followed her over that edge.

She had no idea how long they stood like that, tipped back against the wall with him so deep inside her.

But everything was different now, and so when he recovered himself sufficiently to stand, there was no hint of the Renzo who had taken such care of her in Monaco. That Renzo had carried her to his bath and wiped her gently with a cloth, lest she ache in any way. This Renzo merely set her to the ground and stepped back.

"Two hours," he told her hoarsely. And she did not imagine that the hoarseness in his voice was from the exertion. Not when she could see the dark temper in his eyes. He tucked himself away and zipped himself, and he never shifted that terrible glare from her.

She had lost herself. He had not. She needed to remember that.

"I can't do that," she whispered. "I can't—"

"You will do it," Renzo told her, as if it was a foregone conclusion. "You will call this farce of a wedding off and meet me down in that lane. Or, Sophie, I will teach you a thing or two about consequences."

There were at least two hundred people in the hall, representing almost anyone with any nod toward nobility in all of Europe.

Which was to say, Sophie told herself harshly, these people were not her friends. They weren't here for her. They weren't even here for Dal. This wedding was nothing but a business arrangement, which made the guest list something like…a collection of business associates.

The business they were in was continuing their ancient bloodlines, no matter the cost. And maintaining all the wealth and estates that went with the kind of bloodlines that had been around since the Crusades and in some cases, long before. Standing in the back of the chapel at Langston House, Sophie could pick out any number of couples she'd known forever who had married for similar reasons.

"You will find that our sort of marriages last longer than those predicated on sentiment," her mother had told her when Sophie had failed to entirely hide the emotion on her face at her engagement celebration—a thinly veiled business opportunity for her father and newly minted fiancé. "If you do not give yourself over to false notions of passion and romance, the opiate of the masses and the path to despair if you're not careful, you will discover that a partnership based on shared goals and opportunities is far more secure than any of that other nonsense."

Sophie had been telling herself for years that she believed it.

There was no reason that should claw at her now.

She had waited out those two hours, feeling sicker by the moment. She had done nothing. She had not summoned her father to tell him that things had changed, irrevocably. She hadn't gone to find Dal. She'd run herself a bath and climbed into it, piling her hair on top of her head and letting the steam billow all around her. She'd sunk down deep and sat there so long that if there was water on her face, she couldn't have said whether it was the bath, the heat, or the tears she didn't want to admit she still had it in her to cry.

She thought she might have sat there all day. It felt as if decades had passed. Her skin began to wrinkle and she'd had to run the hot water again and again to keep it warm—but soon enough there was a knock on the door.

Sophie had closed her eyes tight, then opened them. And reminded herself that no one could possibly know that she was faintly swollen and tender between her legs unless she told them—

which she obviously wouldn't do. Of course she wouldn't.

The knocking had come again and she'd made herself call out the appropriate reply, bright and happy the way a bride should sound on her wedding day.

Poppy had come in the way she always did. Bustling, optimistic Poppy, who could make the best of anything.

Even this.

She'd dressed in the adjoining room, a bright salon with breakfast waiting, though Sophie hadn't been hungry. She'd sipped at a strong cup of tea while her hair and makeup had been done. Her bridesmaids had trooped in and out. Her mother had even made an appearance, smiling rigidly at the scene and then excusing herself after the photographer suggested one too many mother-daughter shots.

Because Lady Carmichael-Jones was not sentimental. At all.

It had taken Sophie a while to dress. The wedding gown she'd chosen was wide and long, as classic and traditional as everything else today, and took over the whole of one wall in her dressing room. It was a soft, dreamy white, a lovely complement to how she'd dressed Poppy and the rest in a faint pink, as soft as a whisper, to bring out the coloring that her pretty friend believed she didn't possess.

"You are absolutely beautiful," she'd told Poppy when her friend had come in, fully dressed.

"Don't be silly," Poppy demurred, the way she always did, and had run her hands over the dress that actually suited her curves rather than hiding them. "You're the most beautiful woman anyone has ever seen. Even more so today."

Sophie had only smiled, because she felt a great many things that morning and not one of them made her feel beautiful.

The countdown to two hours had long since passed, and nothing had happened. Renzo had not appeared in all his dark fury. No one had come rushing to the room where Sophie was getting ready to tell her that he had turned up and was shouting horrendous, salacious truths in the middle of Langston House. No one had suggested she look up one of the gossip websites, or had brandished a tabloid.

No one had stopped in to let her know that a

fairly well-known stranger had appeared, uninvited, and demanded that he speak to Dal.

Or worse, her father.

And it was only when she was stepping into her wedding gown and letting Poppy button her into it as if she was tightening the bars on Sophie's cage that she understood that what she was feeling the most was a kind of…disappointment.

She could still feel Renzo between her legs, sweet and stinging faintly from his intense possession.

Perhaps the truth was that she'd expected that to mean something.

After all this, after everything Renzo had done and she had said to him, she still thought he would rescue her.

There was a lesson in this mess, she thought now as the music started. She was already in place down at the end of the long aisle, standing silently beside her father. She could see Poppy standing up before her, down at the altar where Dal waited, looking for all intents and purposes as if he was waiting for a bus. A bus that might in fact have run late, thus mildly inconveniencing him.

That was her groom.

And this is your life, she reminded herself, before she said or did something that might inspire her father to take it upon himself to say something similar.

There was no escape. She'd been foolhardy to imagine otherwise for even a moment.

Her father took her arm and began the long, slow walk, while Sophie tried not to panic about the fact she would be expected to grow old with a man who held her in the kind of esteem he lavished on a bus.

She would have to sleep with him. *Have sex* with him. How had she never thought of that before?

Sophie had considered it in the abstract, of course. But since that night in Monaco, she'd gone out of her way to avoid thinking about that part of things in any kind of detail. Dal would want heirs, naturally. She knew it was part of her job to provide them. And there was only one way she knew to go about doing that.

She tried to imagine Dal taking Renzo's place in any of the things she'd done with him—

But her stomach lurched.

Everyone was standing and looking at her. There were cameras and phones held aloft.

And Sophie's father was walking her down the aisle toward the duty he'd prepared her for since the cradle.

Whether you like it or not, whether your stomach lurches or not, you are going to have to do your duty, she snapped at herself. Here and in the marital bed.

She told herself it couldn't be that bad. Women had been surrendering their bodies to duty and responsibility for centuries and somehow, the world kept turning. It wouldn't kill her to do her part.

Her parents had said as much today.

They had stood with her in the antechamber before the ceremony, standing side by side, both of them tall and trim and perfectly composed. They never touched, Sophie had noticed, the way she always did. Having now experienced sex herself, she didn't entirely believe that they ever had.

"This is a marvelous day for our family," her father had said, sounding as close to jovial as Sophie had ever heard him. Which was to say, he sounded slightly less wooden and disinterested than usual. "I only wish that the former earl had lived long enough to see us merge the families together like this. It's just as we always planned."

"Oh, happy day," Sophie had replied.

And didn't entirely realize how sharp her voice was until she caught the quelling look her mother threw her.

"Pull yourself together, please," Lady Carmichael-Jones had said coolly. Because she was always so cool she might as well have been sculpted from a block of ice. "It would not do to have the new Countess of Langston mewling and carrying on like a common trollop getting married in the back of a pub, would it?"

That was the sort of cutting comment that would normally slice Sophie into bits and leave her tongue-tied and embarrassed. Her mother's specialty.

But Sophie wasn't the person she had been five weeks ago. Or last night.

Or even this morning when she'd woken up.

Oh, no. Now Sophie was exactly what Renzo had made her. What he'd called her and then what he'd showed her she was. Perhaps this was who she'd been all along.

A dark and greedy thing. Selfish. Base and low

and far more of a trollop than her mother could possibly imagine, Sophie was sure.

More to the point, she wasn't afraid of everything the way she'd been before, because the worst had already happened.

It was continuing to happen right now.

"Have you spent a lot of time in the back of pubs, then, Mother?" she'd asked.

The temperature in the antechamber had plummeted.

"Let me be clear, Sophie," her father had said after a moment of silence dragged out into several. Each icier than the last. "My expectation, in case there is some confusion, is that you will acquit yourself appropriately in all things. You were not raised to traipse about the planet, racking up indiscretions and becoming tabloid fodder for housewives in Harrogate to tut over in their local Asda."

"You should consider this an opportunity," her mother had agreed. "To remove yourself from the tiresome social media narrative that seems to have your generation in its claws."

No one waited to see if Sophie was interested in narratives one way or another, she'd noticed.

Much less if she'd like to exclude herself from one of them.

Because none of this was about her. None of this was ever about her.

"When in doubt," her father had told her with great satisfaction, "think of your duty. Family and sacrifice is what has made the Carmichael-Jones family great. It will see you through."

"No matter what comes your way," her mother had added, "and no matter how unpleasant, all you need to do is remember who you are."

On her father's arm now, Sophie walked as slowly as possible down the aisle. As slow as she could without looking as if she was dragging her feet—or making her father look as if he was actually dragging her toward her groom.

She was fairly certain that little speech had been her mother's version of instructing her only daughter to lie back and think of England.

But all Sophie could really think about was Renzo. And how, when she was with him, she thought of nothing at all. Not England. Not sacrifice. Not who she was or wasn't.

Because there was only him. There was only

that dark, addicting magic he spun with his hands. His mouth.

That hard length of him, surging deep inside of her.

But if there was a less appropriate place to think of such things, Sophie couldn't imagine it.

The faces of the guests were a blur around her. Inside, she was nothing but a scream. Loud, long.

But no one could hear her.

No one could ever hear her.

She was the one in the white dress, walking down the aisle toward the altar, the center of everyone's attention—

But she knew perfectly well that no one saw her. Not really.

Only Renzo ever had.

First in Monaco. But this morning here, too.

The man standing there, waiting for her at the end of the aisle, had never seen her. Not the real her. He saw what she represented. Her father's wealth and lands. But she could have been anyone. If Sophie's father had been in possession of sixteen daughters, she knew perfectly well that Dal would have chosen whoever was most expedient, not necessarily Sophie.

It had nothing to do with *her*.

She understood that it never would.

More than that, she understood with a blinding sort of clarity everything she would have to do if she wanted to keep her baby safe in this particular cage she was walking into.

For all her bold talk to Renzo earlier, she actually agreed with him.

Dal might be more ice sculpture than man, but he was still the Earl of Langston. She could not imagine any scenario in which he would knowingly raise another man's child as his.

That meant it was on Sophie to keep her baby safe.

And *that* meant it was also on Sophie to make certain her marital duty was taken care of as soon as possible. A baby might be a few weeks early, but push it a few months and that was begging for trouble.

She tried to visualize it as she moved. She put one foot in front of the other and she forced herself to imagine it.

They would lie down together in a grand bed somewhere as befit an earl. Assuming she didn't immediately contract hypothermia from a single touch of chilly Dal's hand, how bad could it be?

But there was a sinking sensation inside of her, and Sophie had the unpleasant feeling that it could be very, very bad indeed.

Because even if it was unremarkable and indifferent, it still wouldn't be Renzo.

That harsh little truth sank its claws in deep, and tore at her.

But she kept walking.

Her eyes blurred. Her stomach heaved.

Sophie gripped the flowers in her hands so tight she could feel the moisture from the crushed stems making her palms sticky.

And still she walked.

She set her teeth against her tongue and bit down, so she would not say a word. No sobs. No screams. No trollops in pubs.

Just a dignified silence, no matter if it killed her. This wasn't about her anymore. This was about her baby. She would lie back and think of her baby.

England could burn for all she cared, as long as her baby was safe.

Sophie was three-quarters of the way down the aisle when the doors slammed open behind her.

She saw Dal stand at attention, the blank look on his face sharpening.

Next to him, Poppy jolted, and then her face brightened.

"A thousand apologies," she heard Renzo—because of course it was Renzo—drawl out, louder than all the gasps and muttering. "But I am afraid that there has been a change of plans."

Sophie told herself not to move. To pretend it wasn't happening, even as her father dropped her arm and wheeled around.

But she couldn't help herself. She felt…itchy and wild, or maybe she was afraid that she was hallucinating. She didn't know.

And there, three-quarters of the way down the aisle toward the man she'd been promised to when she was still a child, she turned.

She faced Renzo instead.

Renzo, whose eyes were dark amber and hot with rage. And a deep possessiveness that should have terrified her. It didn't. If anything, she welcomed it.

Renzo, who strode toward her, looking for all

the world as if he was out for a quiet, low-key saunter.

Right here in the middle of her wedding.

In the movies, people cried out in moments like these. People leaped up. Everyone reacted, instantly.

But not today. Not here.

Sophie was frozen in place. Her father was beside her, and she could *feel* his scowl, but he didn't move. Around them, lined in all the chapel's pews, there was nothing but shocked silence.

And then Renzo was right there before her.

"I warned you," he murmured.

And then he simply bent, swept Sophie in his arms, and tossed her over his shoulder.

"This is unacceptable!" her father blurted out then.

"This is inevitable," Renzo corrected him, with tremendous calm, as if he wasn't in the middle of abducting a bride from her own wedding. "Accept it now or later, old man. Your choice."

Renzo spun around, making Sophie dizzy, and headed toward the door.

And with every step he took, there was more noise, and not only in Sophie's head.

A voice she thought might belong to her mother, exclaiming, which was something Lady Carmichael-Jones never did, and certainly not in public—

But then Renzo pushed his way through the doors and carried her out into the tremulous summer morning as if he had every right.

He tipped her over again, but only to set her down beside that same low-slung car he'd been driving the night before. He opened the door, then handed her in, and she didn't pretend for a moment that his grip on her arm wasn't anything but an order.

"Do not make me chase you," he told her as he slammed the car door shut.

She was in shock, Sophie thought distantly. Her dress was an impractical layer cake, filling up the interior of the car, flowing over everything. The gearshift. The emergency brake. Most of the console.

She didn't understand until Renzo threw himself into the driver's seat that she could have taken that opportunity to run. To do…*something*. Escape, maybe. Lock him out of his own car, for another. Anything, actually, to indicate that she wasn't on board with being carted out of her own wedding.

But it was too late.

Renzo turned the ignition and the car roared to life.

"I told you what would happen," he bit out.

"So you did."

She didn't sound like herself. But then, if Sophie had learned anything today, it was that she had no idea who she was. Or, to be more accurate, she'd discovered that it was possible she'd never been who she'd imagined herself to be in the first place.

Because surely the proper little heiress, raised from birth to marry the Earl of Langston, would have…fought this.

Struggled, even a little bit.

Instead of what Sophie had done, which was exhale as Renzo had carried her out of that church. As if he'd saved her, after all.

Of course the proper little heiress would likely not have turned up to her own wedding pregnant with another man's child, so there was that.

And now it was done. Even if she tossed herself out of this car at the first turn in the road and ran back to Langston House, the damage was done. There would be no carrying on with the wedding. There would be no pretending this hadn't happened.

There would have to be explanations. And she was still pregnant.

Renzo took a turn too fast on his way out of the Langston estate, exhibiting all the mastery and control that had made him such a star on the racetrack.

He flashed her a look, dark and unreadable, before he took another curve.

And she felt that where she was still tender. She felt it everywhere, inside and out, as if they were connected. As if they were tied up tight to each other with more than just one night in Monaco and an unborn child.

More even than the disrupted wedding of the year.

"Congratulations," Sophie said quietly. "You have well and truly ruined my life."

But Renzo only laughed, that dark shower of sound, male and rough, that made everything worse.

And better, something treacherous whispered inside her.

Because she could feel it.

Sophie could *feel* again, as if that chapel had been antiseptic and gray and this was all sensation and bright color. She didn't know how to process it. She wasn't sure she could.

"I believe I told you I would," Renzo said, and shifted the car into a higher gear, smooth and fast. It felt like a metaphor. And he still had all that laughter in his voice, which was nothing but lightning inside of her, flash after flash. "You are welcome."

CHAPTER SIX

"I HATE TO interrupt this kidnapping," Sophie said mildly when Renzo pulled his sports car onto the tarmac next to his waiting jet at a private airfield outside of London. "But I'm not certain you've thought through the practicalities."

"You will find, *cara*, that I am nothing if not practical. I did not build myself an empire by chance and the liberal application of frothy daydreams."

Renzo didn't wait for her to reply. He was up and out of the car, then moving around the front of it, never taking his eyes off the bridal confection exploding over the front seat of his favorite Bugatti.

It would have helped considerably if Sophie was not *quite* so beautiful, he thought as he moved. Or if, every time he had a taste of her, he didn't simply want more.

More and more, as if she was an addiction.

Renzo had never permitted himself the weakness of addiction, despite the many temptations he'd fielded over the years. Drugs and drink, gambling, women—he'd had a cool head where all were concerned, always. Something spiked and edgy rolled around inside him at the notion that this woman could be what finally changed that.

She's already changed you into a slavering addict, he told himself coldly. *How many other women have you abducted?*

Renzo gritted his teeth, opened the passenger door, and took Sophie's hand to help her climb out of the low, muscular car.

The worst part was, he wasn't immune to the symbolism of the pretty girl in the long white dress, especially as she climbed out of what he had to admit was a particularly masculine sports car. She looked like she should be starring in the wedding he had always assumed he would have one day, if only so he could ensure the legitimacy of the next generation of Crisantis.

No child of his would bear the stigma Renzo had. Not as long as he drew breath.

Of course he had always assumed that he would

choose his own bride. Not that she would present herself, already pregnant and dressed for the part.

But if Renzo had learned anything over the course of his determined climb out of the pit of his humble beginnings, it was that nothing ever went as planned. Ever. He'd learned to accept that and more, to lean into the curves life threw at him, long ago.

It was that or crash.

"Where are we going?" Sophie asked.

Renzo hated her composure. It had slipped a bit, there in that chapel at Langston House. He'd seen a sheen of emotion in her gaze when he'd set her down next to the car outside the wedding ceremony. But with every mile he'd driven her away from her stable little life, she'd recovered her equanimity. Her spine had grown straighter against the back of her seat. Meanwhile, her filmy, gauzy gown had been everywhere, filling up the car. Flowing all over his legs, his lap. Reminding Renzo of what he'd done—what he'd set in stone, with no possibility of changing his mind—with every moment.

Not that he was likely to forget.

"We are going to Sicily, of course," he told her

as he led her across the tarmac. He told himself she needed the help, dressed as she was, but he had the lowering suspicion that despite his towering rage at her attempted betrayal, what he really wanted was to just keep touching her. He cast that aside as he glared at her. "Where, pray, did you imagine I would take the mother of my only child?"

She didn't like it when he called her that, he could see. Something flashed in her gaze, making the gold in all that melting brown gleam a little bit harder. But she only lifted her chin.

"I didn't think you would take me at all. As you must have suspected when you found me halfway down the aisle toward a different groom."

"Did you not? A pity."

His temper had cooled, Renzo realized, and he now felt something very like expansive. At his ease, even. It was because he'd solved the issue at hand, whether Sophie was aware of it or not. There was nothing left but the technicalities. Where they would marry to provide his child with legitimacy. When they would accomplish this. And in between their inevitable wedding and the birth of their child? Well. There was a whole host of punishments he could inflict upon the woman who had walked down that aisle, carrying his child, with every intention of pretending it belonged to another man.

Renzo wouldn't be getting over that anytime soon.

"Perhaps, in time, you will learn that I do not make idle threats."

"Will there be more threats then?" She asked the question brightly, and even smiled that razor-edged, polite smile of hers that no doubt cut England's pedigreed hordes into pieces where they stood. It had a far different effect on him, and all of it located where he was hardest. "That certainly gives me something to look forward to."

Renzo ushered her toward the steps of the plane, unfolded before them, and forced himself to let go of her hand. Because he didn't want to let go of it. Or her. And that was unacceptable.

"It cheers me that you can maintain your sense of humor under such trying circumstances, Sophie," he said when they reached the bottom of the steps. He nodded at his waiting staff, then returned his attention to the woman beside him. "It inspires me to imagine that what lies ahead will not set you back at all. I look forward to this… what do you call it? Your British lip?"

She regarded him for a moment. "A stiff upper lip, presumably?"

"Just so." It was Renzo's turn to smile, and he took it, pleased to see her pulse jump in her throat. "I look forward to seeing it in action in the days to come."

"I am desolated, of course, to throw a monkey wrench in the midst of what sounds like some truly delightful plans." Sophie did not look anything like desolate. She treated him to that smile again, that he imagined women of her class were taught in their finishing schools as a matter of course. "And I certainly do not wish to impugn your manhood, but I don't think you're going to be able to simply pick me up and carry me into a foreign country. It generally requires a passport, for a start."

"The passport you left in your bag," Renzo agreed lazily. "Along with the rest of your luggage, carefully packed for your honeymoon as a countess. Alas, that is a trip you will not be taking."

"You have my passport?"

"I would suggest that you stop underestimating me, Sophie. There will come a time where I will only find it insulting."

"You were…in my room? Going through my things?"

She had started to move while she spoke, climbing the stairs as she held her wedding gown in huge bunches on either side. And still it slipped and spilled everywhere, catching every little hint of breeze.

All he wanted to do was peel it off of her, inch by inch. And then burn it, because it represented the great wrong she had attempted to perpetrate upon him. And while the fire raged, feast on what waited beneath all that soft white fabric.

But she wasn't on the menu at the moment, he reminded himself.

Not quite yet.

Renzo waited until they'd cleared the stairs entirely and had moved inside to the lounge area of his plane. He nodded toward one of the deep, cushy seats and Sophie sank into it, aiming her well-bred frown directly at him.

Because he was supposed to apologize, he imagined, for helping himself to her travel documents and what few garments of hers did not look as if she'd purchased them specifically for her new husband.

"Do you expect me to apologize?" he asked when it appeared she intended to stare at him forever, frown locked in place.

"Certainly not," she said in a tone that conveyed the opposite. "Why apologize for pawing through my belongings? Perhaps that's normal where you come from."

"What is normal?" He took his own seat and lounged back in it, keeping his gaze steady on hers. "Is it—to pick an example at random—giving someone a false name and sneaking off in the middle of the night? Is it summoning them for an illicit meeting in the dark on a deserted country road, but failing to mention the most important piece of information? Or, wait. I know." And Renzo smiled at her then, not nicely, until she jerked slightly where she sat. "Normal must be a woman who finds herself pregnant with one man's child, yet chooses to march herself down the aisle toward another."

"I think you'll find that such things are a whole lot more normal than the fragile egos of men may wish to acknowledge," Sophie said drily.

"Is it my fragile ego you think you have damaged here today?" He raised his brows. "Or, perhaps, it is your grasp of human decency that leaves something to be desired."

Renzo thought she looked pale at that, and her eyes glittered. She made a small production out of folding her hands in her lap, and as she did it she sat a bit straighter. As if she was a queen on a throne, not a bride on the run.

He understood that this was the Carmichael-Jones heiress he was seeing before him now. This was the woman Sophie had been raised to become. Quiet, composed. Perfect for the stale, dry duties of a countess and nothing at all like the wild, half-mad, lustful creature she became when his hands were on her.

Something to file away for later. When he could better take advantage of her weakness, as well as his own.

"Do you have any other objections?" he asked her when she only stared back at him as if her gaze alone could shame him. Little did she know that a man raised in shame chose his path early. Either he lived in shame or became immune to it. Renzo had chosen the latter. And along with it, all those other pointless emotions that governed the lives of others. Love, for example. His father had beaten that out of him, too. "Any other obstacles you imagine you can throw in the path of what cannot be avoided? I invite you to try. Give it your best shot. I assure you, I have thought of everything."

She seemed to take a remarkably long time to moisten her lips, and it turned out he was not immune to that. At all. He shifted in his seat, lest she see the power she had over him.

"How long will we be in Sicily?"

"But that is the best part. Did I not mention it?" Renzo truly enjoyed himself as he let his mouth curve at that. "As long as it takes, Sophie. That is how long we will be in Sicily. As long as it takes."

He wasn't surprised she didn't have much else to say after that. Nor did she ask him to clarify what he meant, because he was certain she didn't want to know.

And he was more than happy to let her stew.

Once the plane was aloft, Sophie excused herself to one of the staterooms. Renzo let her go. He had more than enough business to tend to, as ever, and anyway, he could allow her a little bit of solitude to process what had happened to her this morning. She'd woken to find him right there in her bedroom, confronting her with the scope of her lies and the *consequences*. She'd fought him and then she'd let him take her in a kind of fever, right there against a wall in her fiancé's ancestral home. She'd more than *let* him. She'd been an active, excited participant in that same immolation.

And then she'd gone ahead with her damned wedding anyway. That filled Renzo with pure, unadulterated rage every time he considered it, so he concentrated instead on the part he liked better.

That being when he'd thrown open those chapel doors, strode inside, and taken what was his.

He had never met the Earl of Langston before. Nor any of the well-titled, effortlessly wealthy people who'd attended that wedding. Nonetheless, he'd recognized the type. The big hats and conservative dress of the English peers. The carefully elegant European aristocrats as they'd submitted to another tediously proper ceremony celebrating two of their own. He was vaguely surprised his father wasn't among them in all his princely regalia. By contrast, Renzo was nothing but a beggar at the feast.

But he'd still walked away with the prize.

And there was not one single part of him, the cast-off bastard son of a man very like the people who'd sat in that chapel and tutted their outrage very quietly indeed, that hadn't enjoyed every moment of that.

An enjoyment that would only get better and deeper with time, he was well aware. Because he hadn't simply stolen the Carmichael-Jones heiress away from her destiny. Oh, no. Anyone could have an affair with a dirty commoner and many people in Sophie's nosebleed-high class did. Repeatedly. But in nine months, Sophie would provide this particular cast-off Sicilian bastard with a child, thereby reminding the entire world of the fact she'd permitted him into her sapphire-blue, aristocratic body.

Thereby polluting her haughty, noble blood.

All he needed to do was marry her first, to add insult to injury and make sure that pollution was entirely legitimate.

He was practically jubilant.

And when Sophie did not emerge from the stateroom in what he considered a reasonable amount of time, Renzo went looking for her.

He found her out of her wedding gown at last and showered, with damp hair dripping on her shoulders. She'd changed into some of the clothes he'd packed for her—a pair of trousers that molded to her shapely legs and a soft, desperately fragile sweater in a shade of pale rose that made her seem to glow as she sat there at the foot of the bed.

That was the trouble with Sophie. She was as beautiful here, now, bedraggled and brown eyes wide, as she had been in that wedding gown. Or even that night in Monaco, gleaming as she had in all the bright lights of Monte Carlo.

"Are you hiding?" Renzo asked.

"Of course I am." She gazed back at him, unsmiling, and he found himself unduly taken with the fact her narrow feet were bare, her toenails painted a glossy red. "Is this the part where you gloat?"

He shrugged. "I prefer to do my gloating naked. Otherwise it is less satisfying, you understand."

"So many things to look forward to. I can hardly contain myself."

He handed her what he'd brought for her and watched her reaction as she took it. She blanched, which surprised him. Then held it gingerly before her, as if she expected it to bite.

"I would have thought you would want your mobile," he said, studying her and her reaction. "Desperately, in fact."

She flipped her mobile phone over and over in her hand. "The thing is, you don't actually know anything about me. So I expect you're going to be in for a great many surprises."

"Every socialite I've ever met is attached to her mobile," Renzo said with a certain quiet menace that even he could feel fill the small, compact room. "But of course, you are a special little unicorn, are you not?"

Sophie tossed the phone onto the bed beside her. And if his sardonic tone bothered her, she didn't show it when she fixed that cool brown gaze of hers on him. Very much as if she was the one in charge here.

"Talk me through how this is going to work," she said. It was an order.

Renzo opted not to take the opportunity to show her how very much he objected to being given orders. That, too, could wait.

"Do what I tell you to do," he said instead. "It is as simple as that."

She did not look as if she appreciated his simplicity.

"You've dramatically, theatrically, kidnapped me from my own wedding," she said. "I can't say that I really mind leaving England while all of the fallout from that happens. I imagine it will get ugly."

"It is already ugly." He nodded at her mobile. "You can see for yourself. It's on all the online gossip sites already."

Sophie didn't even glance at the mobile beside her on the bed. She wrinkled up her nose instead.

"And who is more evil in the retelling? You, for storming Langston House? Or me, for allowing you to carry me off?"

"Opinions are split."

"They won't be for long." Sophie's smile was brittle. "I think you'll find that the woman is always, always at fault in these things. No matter what happens. You can expect to be hailed as a great alpha hero while I will be relegated to the role of just another slut in want of a good shaming."

Renzo assumed that was meant to be a slap

at him. What astonished him was that he felt it as such.

"It is not as if you fought to escape me," Renzo pointed out, perhaps a little more harshly than necessary. "You didn't even complain. The truth is that you had no wish to marry that man. I await your expressions of gratitude that I saved you from your fate." His smile felt thin. "Don't flood me with them all at once."

"Whether I wanted to marry him or did not hardly matters."

"It matters to me."

Sophie faltered at that. Then drew herself up. "What matters is that I didn't marry him, after all. The trouble with that is, there were two hundred guests at that wedding and any number of photographers. I'm sure there was a stampede to make it to the tabloids."

"I note that this is your concern." He lounged in the doorway to the stateroom, one shoulder against the doorjamb, as if there wasn't entirely too much of that dark mess he refused to name rumbling around inside him. "I have not heard you mention your earl."

"I am certain that Dal had a moment of concern

over the numerous business enterprises he and my father planned to combine. Just as I'm certain that his first call was to his bank manager."

"This is why I am a romantic," Renzo murmured. "Such love. Such passion. It makes my heart beat faster."

"I don't need you to understand my arrangement with Dal," Sophie said coolly. "What I do need you to understand is that you caused an enormous scandal. That's going to follow both of us." She slid her hand over her belly, which was still the same size Renzo remembered tasting. Repeatedly. It fascinated him that there was a child in there. *His* child. "It will follow this baby around. You understand, don't you? This is something that will never go away."

"And this is a problem…why?"

"Thank you for answering my question, eventually. In a roundabout way." She shook her head. "I'll take all this to mean we'll be staying in Sicily for quite a long time."

"This is not something you need to concern yourself with." Renzo straightened in the doorway. "Your days of merrily skipping around the globe, from this party to that party—"

"I believe you have me confused for some other socialite," Sophie said drily. "Or perhaps an American reality television star. The future Countess of Langston was not a party girl by any estimation. That would have been very seriously frowned upon. Of course, in retrospect, perhaps a party or two would have been better than running out on my own wedding."

"I warned you not to cross me," Renzo reminded her softly. So softly that she flinched a little bit. He watched the tense way she held herself and told himself that what he felt then was triumph. Not that little prickle of the sort of shame he'd thought he'd exorcised years ago. "You could have met me as I asked. You could have canceled your wedding on your own. You chose to make it into a scene instead."

"I don't think I'm the one who made it a scene."

"I gave you the opportunity to take responsibility for what you had done." His voice was gruff, his gaze hot. It felt a little too much like losing control. "You did not take that opportunity. And as you're so fond of consequences, I am sure you will appreciate that there is a price to be paid for that as well."

"So many prices to be paid around you," Sophie said, though she never dropped his gaze. "I can't imagine why you're still single. But then, who could possibly afford you?"

Renzo did not permit himself to lose control. Ever. He had to take a moment to make certain he was not about to do so here. He had been pushed around by far weightier opponents than Sophie Carmichael-Jones, for God's sake. His own father had taught him entirely too many things about his own breaking points. There was no possible way he could allow this woman to wedge herself any further beneath his skin.

Or at the very least, he couldn't let her see that she'd already done it.

"What I care about is the child," Renzo told her when he was certain he could sound appropriately composed. "I enjoy your body, of course. I think you know that."

He liked turning the tables on her a little too much, perhaps. He liked the spots of color that appeared on her face when he said things like that. He liked the way she let out a shuddery sort of breath.

Most of all, he liked the way she held her tongue,

as if she feared that saying something would result in another intense taking, the way it had this morning.

Though perhaps *fear* was not the right word to describe the look in her eyes.

"But I have always had more women than I know what to do with," Renzo continued, and he liked delivering that particular blow most of all. "I cannot imagine any scenario in which I would steal a woman who belongs to another save this one. I would caution you not to read anything personal into it."

"What a shame," she managed to say, her brown eyes glittering with something hectic that he couldn't quite read. "And here I'd planned to start writing you love letters."

"You can make jokes, Sophie. But I know how you sound when you come apart in my hands. I also know that you have never had any man but me. In the days to come, you will likely be tempted to make this something that is not."

"Oh, no," Sophie said, holding his gaze, her own dark with temper. "I don't think that's going to be a problem."

"I'm delighted to hear it. I don't believe in such

emotions. And while you are busy not getting the wrong idea about anything because you are so sophisticated, you are free to consider yourself a surrogate. With benefits."

"I hope that by 'with benefits' you do not mean sex," Sophie bit out at him, bristling where she sat. "Because what happened in Langston House will never happen again. That was the absolute last time—"

"Yes, yes." Renzo didn't exactly roll his eyes, as he was not a teenage girl, but he came close. "You will never touch me again. You are a vestal virgin, made new by the force of your outrage. Spare me the puffed up, Puritan melodrama, if you please. I doubt very much you could resist me if you tried."

"I think you'll find I can. Happily and easily and with joy in my heart."

"You have thus far proven otherwise, *cara*. Repeatedly. When all is said and done, you are an inexperienced little thing who has had the very bad luck to imprint on me while attempting to cheat me out of my own child. Don't imagine that I'm above using it. I'm not above using anything it takes to get exactly what I want."

She surged up from the end of the bed then, her hands in fists at her sides. A better man would not have found that arousing.

Renzo thanked god he was not a better man, by any stretch of the imagination.

"I would be careful if I were you, Renzo," Sophie seethed at him. "If you teach someone how to use a weapon, sooner or later, they'll use it on you."

"I will look forward to that sparring match, then," he said, and waved a dismissive hand, right there in front of her face to make sure she felt sufficiently condescended to. "Back to reality, if you please. You will be my surrogate, with benefits, as I said. And I will promise you one thing. You will beg me to take you. That is inevitable." She looked as if she might pop, so flushed with fury was she then. "But that is merely sex. It is hardly worth discussing. The part I want you to pay particular attention to is this. You will live in my home in Sicily. You will be obedient. If you simply do as you are bid, we will get along famously."

She looked mutinous. "If you say so."

"I'm not a quiet, reserved man, like your earl," Renzo told her, his voice mild enough but the steel beneath it impossible to miss. "I do not suffer in silence. In truth, I do not suffer at all. I have created a life for myself where suffering of any kind is expressly outlawed. I will not put up with any of your antics. You *will* obey."

"Because you don't care if I suffer. Only if you do."

He smiled. "Precisely."

"And what does obedience look like in this delightful prison you've prepared for me?" she asked, her voice a little bit scratchy. To match the temper he could see written all over her, he assumed. "I'm going to need you to lay it all out for me."

"You will meet with my family doctor when we arrive," he told her. Stern and uncompromising. "You will follow his recommendations to the letter. You will be pleasant at all times."

He moved from the doorway then and he liked it when he stepped so close to her that she was forced to tip her head back to meet his eyes. He liked the heat he could see there. The truths that heat told no matter what lies spilled from her lips.

"You have spent all these years practicing how to be elegant. That is what I expect. You have the opportunity to be an aristocratic ornament in my home, Sophie. Do you not feel complimented?"

From the look on her face, she was not only not complimented in the least, she would have torn into him with her fingers if she thought she could get away with it.

"So in your imagination, a pregnant woman will flit about your house, decorously. Not lumber about as I grow big and unwieldy. Is that about it?"

"More or less."

"And should morning sickness overtake me, what then? Is there a place where I can be prettily, obediently sick so as not to distress you with such inelegance?"

"I have a large and well-trained staff, of course. I'm not an animal, Sophie. I'm offended you would imagine otherwise."

"Wonderful. So I'll be trotted out before you only when I am fit to be seen." She studied him for a moment. "Is that how you plan to treat your child?"

He reached over and helped himself to a wet, dark chunk of her hair, curling there against her shoulder. He tugged on it, perhaps not as gently as he might have.

But then, she kept landing blows.

"You don't need to concern yourself with how I will treat the child you tried to take from me," he told her softly. Almost sweetly. "If I were you, I would spend some time learning how to resign myself to the future before you. You will not be returning to England anytime soon. You do not have to worry yourself with whatever scandal we've left behind there today. You've just signed yourself up for nine months in my exclusive company. If I were you, I'd spend a little time contemplating what that means."

"Nine months," she repeated, as if it was a death sentence "And then what? Will you toss me out the door as soon as I'm finished with labor?"

"There will be ample time to figure such things out then," he told her, gazing down at her. That pretty face. Those melting brown eyes with hints of gold. He had to remind himself how little she could be trusted. "Visitation rights, for example, because I am certainly not handing you primary custody of my own child. And little things like when and how to divorce so that it damages the child the least, and causes me as little aggravation as possible."

She blinked. Then frowned. "Divorce?"

"Of course," Renzo said. "You cannot imagine that I would wish to be married forever to a woman who once attempted to steal my child from me and hand it to another man to raise as his? Can you be so foolish?"

She actually laughed at that. "Can *you* be so foolish as to imagine I would ever—*ever*—marry you? You seem to keep glossing this over, Renzo, because you think you know something about me because we had sex. But you ruined my life today."

"Oh, Sophie," he said, and even laughed a little himself. "It amuses me that you imagine you will have a choice. You won't. You had your opportunity to make a choice and you made the wrong one. I will not be so benevolent as to allow it again."

He considered putting his hands on her then and there. He could show her just how easy it would be for him to make her beg him to make use of the benefits he mentioned—but he didn't do it. Not because he had turned into a saint in the course of this flight, God knew, but because he wanted her to fret about it. About all of it.

He wanted this to hurt. The problem with sex when it came to Sophie was that he enjoyed bringing her pleasure a little too much for it to be the punishment he wanted. And he wanted her pleasure more than he should have.

Renzo had no intention whatsoever of acknowledging that. And certainly not to her.

"But—" she began, but cut herself off when he shook his head.

"Look at that," he drawled, and very deliberately thrust his hands in his pockets before they started something he would regret. "You can be taught, after all."

CHAPTER SEVEN

SOPHIE EXPECTED RENZO to force her hand from the start. She steeled herself, expecting him to get in her face again and talk some more about *benefits*.

But once they landed in Sicily and were swept off to the village he called his, he left her to her own devices.

It took her at least a week to understand that it was all part of his design. That, like everything having to do with Renzo, it was part of a greater, diabolical plan.

Because he didn't have to do anything to leave her antsy and worried and half out of her mind with what she chose to call restlessness—and no matter that it seemed chiefly located between her legs. She did it to herself.

Day after day after day.

The village was named after an obscure saint and had been built on a hill, centuries ago. It was a tiny little place, filled with old buildings stacked one on top of the next and winding old roads that seemed to tie themselves in knots as they meandered up and down the steep slopes. The highest building in the town was the old church, named after yet another saint. Opposite it, on a steep slope all its own with sweeping views from the Aeolian Islands to the north to Mount Etna to the south, was a castle that had been built centuries ago by the Saracens and was now a painstakingly restored private home.

When Renzo had called this place *his* village, Sophie discovered, he wasn't being unduly possessive. He'd restored the ancient castle and lived in it like a feudal lord.

The tiny little village that lay at his feet every morning when he woke to gaze down at it was historic, but remote. It was a solid hour and thirty minutes down out of the mountains to Taormina, not that anyone had offered to take Sophie to the only nearby city. Renzo's doctor had been waiting at the castle the day they'd arrived, and had given Sophie a comprehensive physical. He'd pronounced her in excellent health, assured her that the baby was fine, and had promised Renzo—not

Sophie, but Renzo—that he would make weekly visits.

"I don't understand what I'm expected to do here," Sophie said after the first week had dragged by.

She had wandered all over the castle. She had walked the twenty minutes into town, down across a narrow little footbridge that spanned the steep ravine separating the castle from the village. She had spent time in the castle library.

Renzo was sitting behind the desk in the office he kept here. It was a vast suite of rooms, all arching ceilings and astonishing art, with a desk facing a wall of windows over the village. He looked up when she walked in and made a great show of putting down his mobile and fixing his attention on Sophie.

"Is that the point?" she asked. "Do you want to bore me into a coma?"

"You say this as if you normally spend your days neck-deep in industry," Renzo said in that *patience-sorely-tried* voice of his. It made her want to scream. And then he smirked, which only made it worse. "And I do not think that is the case. Unless you spent some quality time digging ditches of which I am unaware?"

Sophie ordered herself not to react. Because she was certain that was what he wanted.

She made herself smile instead. "You don't know me at all, as I keep having to point out to you. I've worked at charities since I left school."

"Ah yes. 'Worked.'"

He made quotation marks with his fingers around the word *worked*, and Sophie had to bite her own tongue to make the red haze of her temper ease back a little bit.

Because she refused—she *refused*—to give him what he wanted.

"I understand you find it hard to believe," she managed to say in as cool a tone as she could manage. "But I actually did work. It's one of the reasons Dal and I had such a long engagement. I didn't wish to be relegated to the ranks of the housewives, wealthy or otherwise, who do nothing but go to the charity parties without doing any of the charity work."

"You have sacrificed so much. Truly. And I'm certain your charitable impulses were in no way a delaying tactic to stave off your wedding for as long as possible."

"I'm sure it means nothing to you," she managed to say without snapping and shouting at him the way she wanted to do, especially as his sardonic tone felt like a torch held too close to her skin. Particularly because he was right, damn him. "But I didn't have a choice about who I was born to any more than you did. However, when my father wanted me to marry at eighteen, I declined."

She didn't tell him how hard that had been. How furious her father had been. How they'd forbidden her from leaving the house for a month as they'd tried to work on her, but she'd held firm.

It had been such a hideous ordeal that it stood to reason she'd been leery of signing up for it again.

Or that was what she'd told herself as her wedding had drawn close.

"I'm shocked that was an option." Renzo sat back in his great leather chair, lounging there with that look on his face that made her hot with something she chose to believe was pure temper. It happened every time he showed how amused he was by her, and how deeply unimpressed. "I was under the impression that you gave your father the mindless obedience you have refused me. That you jumped whenever called."

"I did what I had to do," Sophie said evenly.

She'd walked too far into the room and stood there on the other side of his desk. There were chairs set there behind her, but she didn't take one. She enjoyed the false sense of power she got by standing above him while he sat.

And she had to make her own fun here. With him. Or she feared she would wither away.

"What is your goal here, Renzo?" she asked when it seemed he would be content to simply sit there, watching her as if she was an animal in a zoo. "Do you need me to apologize for every moment of my entire life? I can do that, though I think we both know that that's not actually what you're angry about."

"Perhaps not. But it would make a good start."

"After all," Sophie said, very deliberately, "anyone can see how you suffer. Here in this luxurious castle high on the hill, the lord of all you survey."

Renzo's gaze seemed to light on fire, and Sophie hated that she could feel it *inside* of her. Like flame in her bloodstream and between her legs, a lick of a different fire. He rose from his chair slowly. Deliberately.

And then he was towering above her again, and any advantage she might have imagined she had was lost—but she didn't let herself step back the way she wanted to do. She didn't run.

She held his gaze as if she was daring him to come for her.

Renzo's beautiful mouth hardened. "I lived in squalor. Every day I would walk the streets of this village and dream that one day, I would leave it. As I got older, the dream got more complicated. It wasn't enough to leave this place. I wanted to dominate it."

"I sympathize with the village."

He shook his head at her and the wide desk seemed insufficient, suddenly, to protect her from him. But Sophie ignored that, too.

"I believe you were telling me a very sad story about all you have suffered, were you not?" He looked ready for a fight, sculpted into a dangerous weapon all his own. She didn't know why she imagined she could be the one to give him that fight. "I am prepared to weep openly for you, Sophie. I am certain that any moment now, you will explain to me how your pampered upbringing made the poverty I scrambled about in seem very nearly charming by comparison."

"I was raised for a very specific purpose and that purpose only." Sophie didn't think she was going to convince this man of anything. She didn't know what made her think she ought to try. But she pushed on. "At least you had dreams. I didn't. I was told what my life would be like since I was small."

"Yes, the great tragedy of being raised to become a wealthy, aristocratic countess. My heart bleeds."

"You can mock it all you like," Sophie told him, her voice quiet and her gaze direct. "But that doesn't change it. If I had been a boy, of course, my father would have taught me the family business. But I was a girl, so I was required to marry a man who could handle the business instead."

"You could always have objected. Don't act as if you were helpless." He laughed, in that awful way of his that made everything in her clench tight because she remembered his real laughter. Sunshine and warmth, cascading all over her, making the whole night around them feel like honey, thick and sweet. This laugh just hurt. "A girl like you, everything handed to her on silver platters, is not helpless."

"I'm glad you think so," Sophie threw at him. "If you know so much about my life and how I felt at any given time, why don't you tell me how all this happened? How did I end up here, stranded in a Sicilian castle with a man who hates me? You're the expert, after all."

Renzo laughed again, and it had the same effect on Sophie. But then he moved out from behind the desk and started toward her and that was…worse.

She wanted to stand her ground. She did. But he kept coming, and she found herself backing up. His laugh took on a different note then. Predatory, she thought.

"I'm happy to tell you," Renzo said as he stalked her across the wide floor of his office.

There was something in his dark gaze that made Sophie shake. She had to stop moving to lock her knees against it, but that wasn't any better. That meant he could come much too close.

Then her heart started pounding against her ribs as he began to move around her in a lazy sort of circle, as if he was looking for flaws. And finding them.

"You were born selfish," he murmured, as if these were love words—though he'd told her he didn't believe in such things. Sophie had to fight back a shudder. She concentrated on keeping her fists by her sides. "You were handed advantage after advantage, but never realized how lucky you were. And why would you? You were surrounded by people just like you. I doubt you're even aware that there are people in this world that would kill themselves for an opportunity to face what you consider your problems."

She wondered if he meant people like him—but didn't dare ask. He was behind her then, and she could *feel* him. It was as if he was electrically charged. As if he was his own storm. She could feel her skin shiver into goose bumps because he was there, looking at her. Judging her.

Cutting her down to size.

"Your parents offered you a perfectly acceptable life. You were to be a countess, bathed in even more wealth and status. But that wasn't enough for you, was it?" Was that his breath on her neck? Sophie refused to look. "You needed to create a little excitement for yourself. You needed to make yourself feel better about the life you signed up for with a tiny little rebellion. The one thing you had was your virginity and let me guess—you thought you would seize the opportunity to choose who you would give it to. You thought you would use the only thing that was truly yours."

It was as if he'd been in her head that night, and Sophie felt herself sway on her own feet. How could he know the things she'd told herself? She'd known what he was offering when he'd walked up to her, even before he'd spoken. She'd known that she was expected to keep her virginity for her husband. But she hadn't cared.

Sophie didn't tell him that it wasn't because she'd been hell-bent on a rebellion that night. She hadn't been. By that point, just over a month before her wedding, she'd been nothing if not resigned.

It hadn't been a choose-your-own rebellion. It had been him.

Renzo had looked at her with his face like a fallen angel and she'd decided, in an instant, that he was worth whatever price she would have to pay.

It made her feel light-headed to think of that

now. Here. With him circling her like a dangerous feline coming in for the kill.

"After all, as you keep reminding me, yours was a life without choices," Renzo said, soft and lethal. "That every possible choice you could make was showered with trusts and luxury and glorious estates to cushion the blow hardly signifies, I am sure. You decided you would take it upon yourself to use the only thing you had that you could barter. Your body."

"I'm impressed," Sophie managed to say. She'd crossed her arms at some point, and hugged them to her as if that could contain all the buffeting, conflicting things she felt with every circle he made around her. "It's as if you're psychic. Who knew that in addition to driving very quickly, you could also read minds?"

He only laughed, dark and low, stirring things inside her she didn't entirely understand. Or want to understand.

But the bright, throbbing thing between her legs insisted that she was a liar. That she knew full well what he did to her.

And worse, that she craved it.

"I could have been anyone," he said, and she

caught her breath at the lethal ferocity in his voice then, so close to her ear. She realized that he'd stopped moving and now stood behind her. Above her. Where he could see her and she had to stand there and…guess. "I assume that was your purpose in Monte Carlo. Find a man, betray the promises you'd made, and then smugly attend your own wedding comfortable in the knowledge that one of the gifts you were expected to give to your husband, you'd given away to someone else. How proud you must be."

Her chest was rising and falling too fast, and Sophie was sure he was well aware of it. The way, it seemed, he was aware of everything she'd thought lived only inside her, secret and safe and hidden from view.

But she fought to keep her voice even when she spoke. "I don't understand why, if I was champing at the bit for a chance to fling my virginity at any man who ventured near, I would wait until I was five weeks out from my wedding. And surrounded by friends who would happily report any indiscretions to my fiancé, had they seen them."

"Time was running out." She was certain that Renzo shrugged then, though she didn't see him do it. She had the sense of him there behind her, like a wall. He was that hard. That immovable. "I have known a great many women like you, Sophie. I know you don't want to believe that. I know that deep down, you really do believe that you're a precious little unicorn. All rainbows and butterflies and desperately unique. But I'm afraid you wealthy women are all the same."

"In the dark?" Sophie managed to ask, her voice sharp. "Or do you mean that in a general sense?"

He laughed. "Both."

Because he was Renzo Crisanti, the man who had abducted her from her own wedding. Of course he couldn't be shamed.

"Here's a reality check," Sophie said, aware that there was too much emotion in her throat and that it bled out into her voice. "Men like you might be completely unable to make it through a day without wasting hours upon hours consumed with base, repulsive sexual fantasies. I assume that's eighty percent of what occupies your thoughts at any given time."

She couldn't bear that he was standing behind her any longer and turned, but that wasn't any better. Because he was just as intimidating when she was facing him. More, in fact. Because when she was looking at him it was entirely too easy to get lost in the way he looked. So beautiful it hurt.

And as out of reach as Mount Etna rising in the distance on the other side of his office windows.

Renzo's dark amber gaze blazed in a way that should have given her pause, but she pushed on before he could comment. "Sex was never a factor for me. There were too many expectations put on my behavior for me to even dare think about it too closely. My mother told me, again and again, that anything I did would directly reflect on the family name. And I believed her." She shook her head, trying to clear it. "I was so concerned with accidentally staining my family with a thoughtless act that yes, I was obedient. It must be easy to stand where you are now and mock that. But then, mockery is always easy, isn't it? You should try obedience to one's parents on for size. It isn't easy at all. But it used to be considered a virtue."

That blaze in his eyes was molten now, and she felt as if he was touching her when she knew he wasn't. "A lecture on virtue. From you, of all people. I admit, I am intrigued against my will at the prospect of such brazen hypocrisy."

"It was you, Renzo," she threw at him, fiercely, not caring that her voice was raised and she was making a spectacle of herself. Not caring about anything but telling him how wrong he was about her—as if that would do any good. "I must have seen a thousand men that weekend, but I didn't notice any of them in particular. It was only you who caught my attention. It was only you who really saw me. My mistake is that I thought it meant something."

"It meant so much that you pretended to be someone else. It meant so much that you went into it already lying to me."

"Because you didn't know who I was," she said, the storm in her passed. There was nothing left but the quiet way she said that. And the helplessness she felt, because nothing she said got through to him. The only time she thought he truly saw her now was when he was deep inside her—but that was far too dangerous. "That had never happened to me before. I wanted to be the woman who would meet a stunning man and go off into a beautiful night with him, just once."

He studied her for a long moment. Then another,

while her pulse beat so hard in her veins she was almost afraid they would rupture.

But he didn't react the way she was afraid he might. Or she'd hoped he might, if she was honest. He didn't put his hands on her. And she couldn't read the darkness in his gaze then.

"You asked me for something to do, did you not?"

She had almost forgotten. She swallowed, hard. "Yes. I've been here a week and I'm already going mad."

"Spend more time in the village," Renzo suggested. "Familiarize yourself with the area. After all, at some point you will have to introduce our child to its many joys."

Something shifted between them at that. Sophie couldn't quite place it—and then she understood. He'd said *our* child. Not *his* child, for once.

As if they were in this together.

"People have managed to keep themselves entertained in this village since the dawn of time. I know it can't hold a candle to the many splendors of the London charity circuit, but I suggest you find something here to occupy your days."

"But—"

"Do not ask me again, Sophie," he gritted out. "Because the suggestions I have I do not think you will like."

That sat there a moment, seeming to shimmer in the sunlight that poured through his windows. Or maybe that was the mask he let slip, showing her all that greed and passion that he'd been hiding behind his stony expression and all his terrible words…

"I thought… You said…" The whole world had narrowed to that need in his gaze, and the cast of his sensual mouth, and she felt as if the air had been knocked out of her. "I thought you refused to touch me until I begged."

But Renzo only laughed again, and this was a new laugh.

This one burned her to a crisp and left scorch marks all over her body, she was certain, though she didn't dare take her eyes off of him to check.

"You will beg, Sophie. Believe me, you will beg." He tilted his head to one side and looked at her the way a predator would eye a meal, and she shuddered. "The only question is whether I will let you come to it on your own or whether I will… move the situation along to suit my purposes."

"I… But you…"

"And the longer you stand here, wasting my time, the less inclined I am to wait."

Sophie stopped pretending that she could stand up to this man. She turned on her heel and bolted from the room, that dark, stirring laughter of his following her down the halls of the castle as she fled.

CHAPTER EIGHT

SOPHIE SPENT THE next week exploring the village, but not because she wanted to one day give her baby a tour of the place. She was looking for a way out.

"There is only one bus in my village," Renzo had told her on the drive from the airfield, down near the sea, the day they'd arrived in Sicily. "It leaves very early in the morning on market days and returns after dark, and that is only when the driver remembers to come all the way up the mountain. You should also know that the driver and his large family live in a house I own."

Sophie had been staring out her window at the sun-drenched landscape, unable to fully process the fact that she'd woken up that morning in Hampshire, prepared to marry Dal, and was now on the far side of Europe with a man she kept sleeping with, who was not Dal. At all.

"Why would I need to know any of that?" she'd asked.

"Because, *cara*," he'd said in that way of his, as if he was creating intimacy every time he looked at her. "One day you will wake up and decide you wish to escape my hospitality. On that day, it will save us all a lot of trouble if you remember these small facts. There is one sporadic bus. Everyone on it will be loyal to me, especially the driver. You will get nowhere."

She'd looked at him then, across the expanse of the backseat they shared, and had wondered how he managed to be awful at every turn and yet her heart still flipped inside her chest whenever she looked at him. What was *wrong* with her?

Had she really thrown away her whole life for… this?

"Thank you," she'd said stiffly. "I'll be sure to keep that in mind. While walking."

Renzo had smiled, looking something like benevolent, which had been her warning.

"The village is perched on a little stretch of land propped up between many steep ravines," he'd told her. "People fall down them all the time and die, especially in the ice and snow of winter, but they are in many ways more treacherous in the summer. The road is narrow and very curvy. Pedestrians are forever walking on that road and getting struck by vehicles taking the turns too fast. It's also a solid, steep hour's walk to the next little town, assuming you aren't hit by a car on the way. I can't say I recommend it."

Sophie spent her second week in Sicily discovering that nothing Renzo had said to her that day was an exaggeration. The road out of town was terrifying. It shot down from the lowest part of the village in a steep, near-vertical drop, then began to curve this way and that. No matter how many times Sophie girded her loins and determined she would walk it anyway, she stopped the moment she saw a car careen up or down, promising certain death.

She wanted to get away from Renzo. But she certainly didn't want to die.

The bus situation was even worse than he'd claimed. The women in the village shrugged and seemed not to know when it might run again. One cited vague "troubles" that Sophie thought might involve the driver's personal life rather than his vehicle, not that anyone appeared to mind that much.

There were no cars for hire. Or no cars for her to hire, anyway.

The locals were friendly. They greeted her with smiles, and happy chatter, but she quickly realized that there was a limit to that friendliness. And that limit was Renzo.

"How much would it cost to get to the airport?" she asked the man with the only taxi she had been able to find in town one warm afternoon.

The man started to quote a number, but then stopped. He eyed her.

Summer in Sicily was hot and sunny all day, then cool at night. The little village had a lovely, sunlit square, with shade trees all around where the old men sat and whiled the days away. And the taxi driver stared at her so long, Sophie was glad they'd stepped out of the direct sunlight.

"Surely *il capo* can take you to the airport when he is ready, no?" the driver asked. That was what they called Renzo here, she'd learned. *The boss.*

"I wasn't planning to ask him," Sophie confessed, and smiled as brightly as she could.

But the driver was unmoved. "I couldn't take

you to the airport," he told her, definitively. "Or anywhere. It would not be possible."

"But I can pay you," she assured him. "Double. Triple, even."

The driver shook his head. Then he held up his hands and backed away, as if Sophie was threatening him.

The way the rest of the villagers looked at her, it was as if they thought she really had.

And when she made her way back up the hill and over the ravine—that was a steep shot down so far it made her dizzy to look over the edge of the footbridge—she found Renzo waiting for her in the castle's grand hall.

She didn't say anything. Or couldn't, to be more precise. He was dressed in a dark suit that suggested he'd been conducting video meetings from his office with his employees around the world, and she felt grubby by comparison in the hiking shorts and T-shirt she'd thrown on—selections that had been waiting for her in the closet of her rooms here when she'd arrived. She'd opted not to think too closely about where they'd come from.

"Do you know why there is a castle here?" Renzo asked mildly.

It was the mildness that got her back up. “Because there’s a marvelous view?”

“Yes,” he agreed. “But back when men roamed the land and built castles, the kinds of views they were looking for were oriented in defense, not leisure. This village is perfectly situated to defend itself against all comers. There is only the one road in and out. It is bordered by cliffs all around. No one can sneak up on this place. Few try.”

He didn’t say, *And also no one can leave*, but Sophie got his meaning.

“Come,” he invited her, in that low way of his that was not an invitation so much as it was an order. “We will sit, you and I. We will have a conversation like civilized people and you will tell me, Sophie, how it is you imagine you can escape me so easily.”

His lips curved at her expression of shock, though she’d tried to conceal it.

“The taxi driver you attempted to enlist to betray me called to tell me of your perfidy.” Renzo made a *tsk*-ing sound. He might as well have scraped his fingernails down her spine. She glared at him, but that only made his smile deepen. “You will find that betraying me will not come quite so easily as betraying your earl."

"I wasn't trying to betray you," Sophie said tightly. "I was trying to get a ride to the airport. They're not the same thing."

"Where do you imagine you can go?" he asked, almost as if he really wanted an answer to the question. But then his eyes flashed. "I will find you wherever you run. You must know this."

She cast around for some kind of defense, but she didn't have one. He would view any attempt she made to leave him a betrayal. And she knew that, didn't she? There was no sense pretending she didn't know exactly how he'd react to her leaving. Or even any attempt on her part to leave.

Isn't that what you wanted? something in her asked, wicked and knowing. *Isn't that what you've always wanted from him? His reaction?*

Renzo led her into the library, a glorious room that made Sophie's heart ache a little every time she entered it. Beautiful books lined the walls. There was a fireplace on one side and French doors on the other that opened into a kind of sunroom and then, beyond that, a terrace with views that stretched all the way to the Mediterranean.

Inside, there was a great, raised skylight that let the sunlight in and highlighted the many armchairs and couches scattered about, all of which she'd tried at different points during her forced Sicilian holiday.

But this afternoon she followed Renzo to a little cluster of seats before the unlit fireplace, and tried to read his mood as he settled himself across from her.

He usually dressed simply here. A T-shirt and trousers, which should have looked casual but didn't, somehow. It wasn't simply the excellence of the fabrics he chose, though Sophie was certain that played a part. It was Renzo himself. He was not a casual man. Even his casual clothing failed to take away from his intensity in any way.

And today he was not wearing a T-shirt and trousers, like a normal man. He was dressed to emphasize his power rather than dampen it.

It ricocheted inside of Sophie like a bullet, and all he did was sit there.

Looking at him made her palms feel itchy. Sophie rubbed them on her thighs, but then stopped when she saw the way Renzo tracked the movement, as if it was evidence he could use against her.

"You persist in failing to understand your situation," he said after a moment, his tone almost absent, as if he was speaking to a troublesome employee. There was no reason that should slap at her, Sophie told herself, when it was the least of the things he'd done to her. "What about this is confusing?"

"Do you really want to keep me in prison?" she asked, and she had no idea why there was so much emotion in her voice, making it sound so rough. "Am I expected to sit quietly in a room somewhere, staring at the wall?"

"I told you to find something to do in the village. Or is the simplicity of village life too far below a woman of your exalted standards?"

Again, that sardonic tone he used like a lash.

"You don't have to insult me every time we speak," Sophie managed to say without giving in to those emotions that still slopped around inside of her. "Would the world end if you were nice to me for five minutes?"

"There is one way that I'm more than happy to

be nice to you," Renzo said, and his voice changed again.

And Sophie caught fire.

"I want you to tell me how it is you think I should spend my time," she said, very deliberately. She wasn't going to touch the sexual innuendo part of the conversation. She had no idea what she might say.

Or worse, *do*.

"You do not, apparently, know how to entertain yourself. Is that what I'm hearing? Again?"

"I'm perfectly capable of entertaining myself," Sophie snapped at him. "I've read a lot of books. I've taken a lot of walks. It's been two weeks and I've seen everything there is to see, twice. What I can't get my head around is what I'm meant to do for the next nine months."

Renzo lounged there in the chair across from her, wicked and angelic at once, mouthwateringly ruthless in all things, and the way he looked at her then was…unfair.

"As it happens," he murmured. "I have an opening."

Something about his tone sneaked down her neck and along her spine, making her too aware of him. All of him. That gleam in his dark eyes and that curve on his hard mouth. The way he sprawled there, his legs thrust out before him. There was something about the way this man's body affected her that made her want to cry. He filled her with despair, wild and huge and overwhelming.

Though Sophie didn't think that was the correct word for the things she felt when she gazed at him.

It was easier to call it *despair* than it was to interrogate the parts of her that pulled tight and greedy, hot and nearly painful, every time he was near.

And there was something about the way he was looking at her this afternoon that made it that much worse than it normally was.

"A position in your business?" she asked.

"My business?" He laughed at that. "You have already told me your résumé, Sophie. I expect you know it is not exactly impressive. You were raised to be a dilettante and lived up to all expectations. What use could I possibly have for that?"

What she would have to sort out later, when she was alone, was why she was always surprised by his sucker punch. He landed it every time.

Sophie couldn't blame him—it was clearly just what he did.

Why did she persist in imagining he could ever be the man she'd imagined he was that first night?

"Thank you," she said quietly, after a moment. "For always making certain that I know exactly who you are. That I'm not tempted, for even a minute, to forget."

"I do like to be memorable," Renzo said.

"I'll have to consult the internet when I have a moment," she said, shifting slightly in her seat so she could hold his gaze, her chin tipped up. "But I'm fairly certain your résumé is even less impressive than mine. Car races and a handful of high-profile affairs with actresses in the first rung of their downward spiral, if I remember correctly. And a few hotels and clubs thrown in to diversify your portfolio, of course."

If she thought she could land a similar punch on him, she was mistaken. He only smiled.

Like a wolf.

"Don't worry, the position I have in mind is more firmly in your skill set."

Sophie knew, somehow. It was the way he was looking at her. Less frozen than it had been these last two weeks, for a start. It was the way the air seemed to tighten between them, complex and complicated, thick and textured—and yet very, very simple.

"I'm afraid to ask what you think my skill set is," she said.

"I want you to do what you do best, *cara*." There was something wrong with his voice, then. It was raw. Too dark. It worked its way through her like a roll of thunder. "I am not in need of another secretary. Or an office girl of any description."

"My talent is in running things," she told him, which was true enough, though she doubted he cared. "I have my own support staff."

"I don't require you to run anything," Renzo told her, his dark amber gaze lit with a fire that made her feel lit up and hollow at once. "Or support anything. But in these halcyon days before our inevitable wedding and the birth of our child, I do find myself very interested in a new mistress."

"A new mistress."

Sophie repeated his words as if they were in a language she didn't speak. As if they made no sense to her, when Renzo could see that she understood him perfectly.

He could see it in the flush that worked its way down her neck to flirt with the scoop neck of the casual shirt she wore. He could tell by the way she crossed and uncrossed those long, shapely legs of hers, shown to advantage in the shorts she wore that had him longing to reacquaint himself with every last inch of them.

She was driving him to distraction. And he was tired of talking about it. He was tired of catching her scent in the halls when he least expected it. He was tired of being haunted by her the way he had been all those weeks when she'd disappeared and taken her fake name with her.

And this time, he didn't have to wait for an enraging clipping from a foreign newspaper to find her again. This time, she was right here.

He was tired of pretending he wanted anything but to bury himself inside her until he tired of her, assuming that day ever came.

"Surely you know what mistresses are, Sophie," he said, a little too much aggression in his voice. And that was him trying to control himself. "I would think that in your world, particularly, there are more mistresses than there are wives. If perhaps not all in the same place."

She smiled, but he thought it looked forced. "*Mistress* is such a funny word. Do you mean you just want sex? Is this just how you hit on the women you strand in your castle? You can see why I'm confused. After all, it's not the seventeenth century."

"Of course I want sex, and quite a lot of it," Renzo said, and the way he said it was deliberate. He wanted her to feel silly. Inexperienced and virginal, and he could see she did in the way she blushed. Then dropped her gaze. "But the role of a mistress is well defined. There are no…unreasonable expectations. Everyone involved knows the terms, and there is no deviation from them."

"That sounds depressingly corporate."

"But that is the point, Sophie. It is not romantic at all. It is an exchange. In your world, I believe engagements from the cradle serve a similar purpose, though they are perhaps less physical. Here, you will get what you want and so will I. No drama. No hurt feelings. No tears."

"You think the word *mistress* is magical enough to prevent all of that?"

"I do," he said. He watched her closely. "Because it's a contract, not a fairy tale."

Much as their marriage would be, given that it was only for the child's legitimacy. He would have no confusion on that score, either—but there was no need to get into that with her now. This was a good first step.

He watched her swallow hard, as if her throat was dry. Her lush lower lip trembled slightly, until she pressed her lips together. She took her time threading her fingers together in front of her, and only then did she raise her gaze to his again.

"What is it you want from a mistress?" she asked. And then, when he let his mouth curve, she hurried on. "Sex, obviously. I'm not sure why, if that's what you want, you have to go to such absurd lengths to make it a transaction."

He forced himself to lounge back against his chair when every part of him was hot. Ready.

"Because I can get sex anywhere," he told her without a shred of conceit. Because it was a fact. "It is thrown at me when I walk down the street. It is everywhere I go."

"My condolences."

He liked when she showed her fangs, and

smiled. "But this is the problem, you understand. Simply because a beautiful woman looks at me in a certain way on the street, for example, this doesn't mean that we will suit each other in bed. And let's say that we do suit." Renzo shrugged, though he never shifted his intent gaze from her flushed face. "How do I know she will not make the grave mistake of falling in love with me? Because I do not allow love to pollute my relationships, Sophie. Ever."

"Is that really a concern?" Sophie asked, and her voice was still clipped. Her brown eyes glittered and he thought, whether she knew it or not, his little captive was jealous. "Because I have to tell you, I really don't think that's as much of a factor as you seem to imagine."

"Says the woman who is soaking wet right now, sitting across from me in a library."

He watched her cheeks blaze with heat. She pulled in a sharp breath, and her hands gripped the arms of her chair as if she didn't know whether to run for it or take a swing at him.

And he doubted she was aware that the scent of her arousal hung between them, telling him everything he needed to know.

"I'm not surprised you have a vacancy," she said after a moment, though he was pleased to hear she sounded breathless. "You don't make the position sound very appealing."

Renzo stretched, and enjoyed the way she watched him. As if he was a dessert and she couldn't quite keep herself from taking a little lick. He shifted forward, putting his elbows on his knees and letting his hands dangle in front of him.

The tips of his fingers brushed her bare knees.

Once, then again.

She caught her breath, then let it out in a sigh that sounded a whole lot like surrender.

"Just think, Sophie, if all of this was set aside," he said softly. "The silly games. The outraged posturing. Imagine if all you had to think about was greeting me just as you are, slick between the legs and nipples hard as rocks, with no thought in your head but our mutual satisfaction. Think how quickly these nine months would go if that was your only focus."

For a moment, she imagined it. He could tell by the way her eyes went unfocused. The way her mouth fell open, just slightly. He could see the color on her cheeks and the wild drumming of the pulse in her throat.

He could imagine it too easily. Every day could be like that night in Monaco. She would give herself to him, again and again, and this time, he wouldn't have to worry about losing her every time he went to sleep.

Are you worried about losing her or are you concerned she'll try to call this love? he asked himself. And couldn't seem to find an answer.

Before him, sitting too straight in her chair, Sophie shook herself.

"Don't be silly," she said, sounding particularly British and scolding. He assumed it was as much for her benefit as it was for his. "I can't just…be your sex slave."

"Why not?"

Sophie's pupils dilated. Renzo leaned forward a little more and traced patterns on the bare skin before him. Her knee, again. Then down along the leg she'd crossed over its mate, as if he was drawing patterns on her taut, satiny flesh.

He was so hard it hurt.

"I'm glad this is a joke to you," she said. Weakly.

"I'm not joking at all." Renzo leaned forward

and slid his hands onto her lap, relishing the way she bit back a sound at that. It reminded him of the way she came, and he nearly lost his composure. It took him far too much work to pull himself together, but he managed it, though his jaw ached from the way he clenched his teeth. "Here's the problem, *cara*. You can, if you wish, waste your months here traipsing around the village entreating my people to do your bidding. They won't."

"What do you mean, *your people*? This isn't a feudal estate."

He trapped her hands in his and held them, angling himself even closer.

"It might as well be. This village was falling down when I left it at eighteen. No industry to speak of. Goatherds and shopkeepers were the lucky ones. Everyone else was simply trapped here, the way their families have been for generations. But I changed all that."

He turned over one of her hands and examined it, noting the ragged nails that suggested she'd developed her own nervous habits while she'd been here. *Good.* He could only hope he drove her half as crazy as she did him.

"I didn't merely take over all the leases and

mortgages I could and fix up all the falling-down buildings. I bought the hotel over the next ridge and I financed it with my own money for the first five years, so it didn't matter if the tourists came or not. But they came." He looked at her other hand and reveled in the deep tremor he could feel go through her. "This village may be sleepy but the hotel is successful, and between it and the connected vineyard, I employ the bulk of the villagers."

"I had no idea you had a single humanitarian bone in your body. I'm shocked."

"What I am trying to tell you, *cara mia*, is that there is not a single person living here who is not aware of the hand that feeds them. They will not cross me. No matter how you smile or bat your eyelashes, you are trapped here. But then, you have been at pains to tell me that you have always been trapped, so perhaps it is not so much of an adjustment."

She worried her lip with her teeth for a moment, then stopped as if she knew how it felt inside him. How it made him ache to test that lip with his own teeth. "I suppose it's good to know that you're capable of kindness, anyway. Even if you feel no particular compunction to show it to me."

"You are the one who asked me for something to do with your time," he reminded her.

Sophie sat a little straighter, and her brown eyes were too dark. "I've never been asked to be someone's mistress before."

"Good," he growled, before he could think better of it.

"I'm fairly certain that the appropriate response is outrage."

What Renzo noticed was that she didn't look outraged at all. And she didn't try to wrestle her hands from his. "What is there to be outraged about?"

"Oh, you know. The stain on my character and how little you must think of me to suggest such a thing. Small, inconsequential things like that."

"Tell the truth," Renzo murmured, dark and urgent. "How often do you wake in the night, wishing I was there beside you? I make you hungry. I make you wet and restless. You torture yourself with memories of how good it is between us. You fall asleep and dream of that night in Monaco and all the ways I filled you and took you and made you mine." She let out a soft little sound, not quite a moan, and it took everything he had not to simply reach over and haul her into his lap. "I see no reason to play these games of make-believe when we both know the truth."

She looked as if she might faint. She tugged on her hands, but when he released them, her expression seemed…crestfallen.

"You can't just go around asking people to be your mistress," she said faintly.

"I'm not asking *people*. I'm asking you."

It occurred to him that he was entirely too invested in her answer, and not only because he was so hard it bordered on pain. And it was that other part that concerned him. He reminded himself who she was. What she'd done.

But when he conjured up visions of Sophie in that filmy confection of a wedding gown, walking down the aisle, it wasn't betrayal he thought of.

In his head, she was making her way down that aisle to him.

That rocked him to his bones. It shook through him like a revelation, dark and terrible. Renzo released her and sat back, then made himself lounge as if he'd never been more relaxed in his life.

"And I'm not really asking you, to be perfectly clear," he heard himself say, cold and impersonal again, the way he should have been all this time. "I'm telling you that the position is open and you can do with that information anything you wish."

Sophie blinked, then went a little pale again. But he didn't let the gnawing thing inside him get to him. He had never been a soft man and he didn't know why there was something in him that wanted nothing more than to bring that color back to her face.

He had the sinking sensation that he was in this much, much deeper than he wanted to admit.

And he had no idea what to do about that.

"Your suite of rooms is directly next to mine," Renzo told her, and he couldn't seem to control his voice anymore. He sounded gruff. He felt… wrecked. "The door is never locked. When you are ready to take on your new role, all you need to do is open that door and walk through it. What could be simpler?"

She regarded him for so long, so quietly, that he started to feel something like panic work its way through him—

Though that was impossible, of course. He was

Renzo Crisanti. Lesser men panicked. Renzo conquered.

"What if I never walk through that door?" she asked.

Renzo made himself smile and elected not to notice how difficult it was.

He studied her as she sat there before him. He saw the way she trembled a little bit. The way she kept her mouth shut tight as if she was afraid of the things that might come out of it if she opened it.

At least if this was getting to him, it was getting to her, too.

"It's up to you," he told her. "But as in all things, there are consequences. The longer you take, the more I will demand. It is inevitable."

"Consequences," she whispered. "There are always consequences."

"Always," Renzo agreed.

He thought he was handling himself admirably when he kept his hands to himself. When he only sat there as if he didn't care either way what she chose, when he was rapidly coming to the conclusion that he did. He really did, and he had no place to put that to make any sense of it.

"But the good news for you, Sophie, is that I don't just want to make you pay," he told her, and he had the pleasure of watching those big brown eyes of hers widen, all golden heat, because however hard this was for him, it was harder for her. As it should be. That was why he smiled. "First I want to make you scream."

CHAPTER NINE

IT TURNED OUT that having choices was harder, Sophie discovered, and no matter what her mother might once have said about *poor people*. Because she was the only one she'd have to blame once she made them.

Renzo storming into her wedding and carrying her out, tossed over his shoulder as if he was some kind of ancient marauder, was easy because it allowed her to hold him accountable. *She* had intended to marry Dal, as promised. *She* had never meant any of this to happen, so how could she be held responsible for something Renzo had done?

She thought a whole lot about that after Renzo left her there in the library, while she tried—and failed—to catch her breath. Right there, in the chair where he'd left her, that enigmatic look on his dark face and entirely too much carnal promise in his gaze.

Of course she couldn't agree to be his mistress, she told herself stoutly. She was outraged that he'd even suggested such a thing, especially when he kept threatening to marry her in the same breath—

But maybe that was the trouble, she thought a bit later, when she'd showered off her walk and found herself sitting in her bedroom. It was furnished with exquisite antiques and a canopy bed she doubted she'd ever get a good night's sleep in again, after all the images Renzo had put in her head. The sun was beginning to lower in the sky over another day in Sicily, and everything was exactly the same as it had been the day she'd arrived, except her baby was a bit bigger inside of her.

She slid her hands over her belly, imagining that she could already feel a difference. And she wasn't quite as outraged at Renzo's suggestion as she thought she ought to have been.

Sophie had tossed her mobile in the drawer of the bedside table without looking at it the day they'd arrived, and she hadn't touched it since. But the word *responsibility* was dancing around and around in her head tonight, so she went and got it out, frowning down at the thing as she switched it on.

Sophie hadn't wanted to look. She'd spent two weeks with her head thrust firmly in the sand, because she'd been certain that she didn't want to know anything that was happening in the world Renzo had carried her away from.

Which is just another way to avoid taking responsibility for yourself, isn't it? a caustic voice inside her asked.

The truth was that she very much doubted that she had anything to go home to, even if she could manage to escape this remote village.

And when she started going through all the notifications on her mobile, it was as bad as she'd imagined. Worse.

Sophie had too many voice mail messages. Entirely too many texts. Some people she'd called friends for lack of a better term had sent her links to tabloid articles shredding her to pieces, which was helpful, in the long run. Because it reminded her how few real, true friends she'd ever had.

There was only one, by her estimation. Poppy. Sweet, dependable Poppy, who was the only person Sophie wanted to talk to at all. Because she was well aware that she'd left Poppy to deal with

Dal, which couldn't have been pleasant—especially since Poppy worked for him.

But she couldn't seem to reach Poppy, which only made her feel worse.

And everything else was character assassination and innuendo. Or outright hostility.

"Don't bother to contact us, Sophie," her father said in the last of the numerous messages he'd left for her, each one more vicious than the one before. "You have tarnished the family name beyond repair. I hope your tawdry affair is worth it."

Sophie knew exactly what lay ahead for her, if she went back to London. She'd seen more than one girl who'd been raised the way she had, complete with a shiny pedestal all her own, who had then fallen straight off. She knew how it went. Some rehabilitated themselves eventually, usually after years of intense publicity campaigns—though that would never satisfy some of the bigger snobs. Some simply made lateral moves into different marriages, though Sophie had always thought privately that said lateral marriages must be even worse than the ones they might have had before.

Because it was one thing to be virtuous and untouched and worthy of one's chilly arranged marriage. It was something else again to be damaged goods.

Just one more concern specific to her exalted position, Sophie knew. Girls without estates attached to their name and trusts that stretched back to the condescension of ancient kings had all kinds of choices. They could do as they pleased. They could marry for love, sow their wild oats as they liked, make their life anything they wanted it to be without concerning themselves with a highly polished family name.

Sophie had never had that choice. She'd never had those options.

But you have a choice now, that same little voice reminded her.

She had no doubt that Renzo would push the legitimacy issue and the marriage he wanted. Her choice was simple—did she want to spend the time before that inevitable marriage and her child's birth the way she'd spent the past two weeks? Or did she want what he was offering instead?

Sophie had made one other decision about the course of her life, and it was what had brought her here. She'd taken one look at Renzo and had wanted him. He was the only thing she could remember wanting—because she'd learned a long time ago that there was no use wanting things she couldn't have.

But she could have him now.

He'd said as much.

All she had to do was walk through that door on the wall nearest her bed that she hadn't realized was only locked on her side…

Mistress. She turned the word over again and again in her head.

He'd called it a practical arrangement. Sophie couldn't help thinking it was begging for trouble. It had been hard enough to walk away from him that night in Monaco. She'd watched him sleep as she'd dressed, feeling as if she was torn into pieces. How could she go back to her black-and-white life, so cold and precisely contoured to other people's specifications? How could she live in all that dark and gloom when she'd finally felt all that sunlight on her face?

But she'd made herself leave anyway, because she'd thought it was the right thing to do.

It had been hard after one night. What did she think it would be like after months? And a child?

Sophie threw her mobile back in the drawer, feeling much more unsettled than she had when she'd picked it up. She didn't bother to call her parents back, because she knew them too well. If she called now, there would be nothing but recriminations. Accusations and harsh words. If she waited, they would retreat into their usual icy hauteur. They always did. And that would be the best time to tell them that they had a grandchild on the way.

Because at the end of the day, her parents were nothing if not practical. The sooner she told him they had a grandchild on the way, the sooner they could start plotting out more dynasties. Which was, as far she could tell, the only time they were ever happy.

Or as close to happy as they ever got.

That night, she lay in her canopied bed, completely unable to sleep.

All she could seem to do was stare at that door on the wall. The only thing she could concentrate on was Renzo lying there, in his bed, just the way she was. Would he be naked? All that sculpted muscle there between his sheets with no other barriers? Was he lying awake just as she was, watching the door? Or was he asleep?

If she slipped through to his rooms, could she make it to the side of his bed before he knew she was there? Would he reach for her?

Or would she crawl over him, and get to revel in another moment of watching him as he slept?

The way she had that morning in Monaco before she'd run back to her life, guilty and ashamed by the things she done and let him do in turn.

"If doing it one night—and one morning—made you feel so guilty and ashamed," she said out loud, her voice sounding strained and strange in the dark room, "why would you do more of it? As an *arrangement*?"

She didn't feel as if she'd slept at all, and when she woke, the light was streaming into her room. It told her she'd stayed in bed much later than she usually did.

When she finally dressed and made her way down to the breakfast room—where there was always coffee, freshly baked pastries, and a soothing view of mountains stretching toward the sea in the distance—she stopped short, because Renzo was there.

"You look as if you didn't get much sleep," he murmured, that damned curve to his mouth and those dark amber eyes all over her. "Whatever could have kept you up? Tossing and turning? Too hot, perhaps?"

"Not at all." She had stopped in the door to the bright little room set over a sweeping balcony and she couldn't seem to make her feet move another inch. So instead, she smiled wide and lied some more. "I'm not sure I've ever had such a deep sleep."

Renzo's gaze lit with amusement. He didn't call her a liar. But then, he didn't have to.

"Have you come to a decision?" he asked instead.

Sophie forced herself to move, then. She walked over to the sideboard where the staff had prepared the usual trays of breakfast treats and selected the traditional Sicilian summer breakfast she'd come to crave each morning, sweet brioche and almond granita, which the locals ate in some form or another to ease into the hot mornings. And an extra strong small cup of espresso, because lord knew she needed that and then some to handle Renzo's unexpected presence after having him in her head all night.

"I love the brioche here," she said, as if that was the decision he'd asked about. "And of course I love it with gelato, but that's a bit heavier than the granita, isn't it?"

"That is, of course, the question I wanted answered. Your breakfast options are an enduring fascination to me. Thank you."

She settled herself across from him at the small table as if that was normal. As if they ate together every day. And she fought to keep her expression bland when she met his too-knowing, too-amused gaze.

Something moved in her then, a little too hot, as she imagined this might be part of the arrangement if she agreed to be his mistress. Instead of having him in her head all night, she would really, truly have him, and then...would they share meals like this? Would he stop treating her with all that barely contained ferocity?

Would he forgive her for what she'd planned to do with their baby?

Will you forgive yourself? a voice from somewhere deep inside asked her then, with a certain quiet savagery that left her reeling.

The question fell through her like a blow. A series of blows, each more brutal than the last. Like shattering glass, leaving marks as it went.

And Sophie didn't know what to do with any of it, so she let her granita melt as she stared at the man across from her.

"I don't understand what makes you think that calling me a mistress would somehow take away all the intimacy of the arrangement," she blurted out. If she'd had the time or capacity to think it through, she wouldn't have said anything and she certainly wouldn't have used that word.

Mistress. It sat there between them like a sexual act. Or maybe that was just how it felt to Sophie. It was so…debauched. Erotic, but wrapped up in such a staid and sturdy little word.

"It is an arrangement that is entirely about sex," Renzo said, and his dark, rich voice didn't help matters. "It is necessarily intimate. What it is not, *cara*, is emotional."

"I don't know why you imagine emotions are something you can order about the way you do everything else," she said, with a little too much of her own feelings on display.

She regretted it instantly. The way she regretted everything that had to do with this man.

Liar, whispered that voice again, and she actually shuddered this time.

Renzo saw, of course. He saw everything. She watched his gaze shift from that amused heat to something darker. Something unreadable.

"I can't help you with this, Sophie," he told her after a moment. He was not wearing one of his dark king-of-the-universe suits today. That meant she could see far too much of his sculpted biceps beneath the material of his T-shirt. And the strong, golden column of his throat. And entirely too much of his beautiful chest. He was distracting. But he was still talking, and for once he didn't sound ferocious—he simply sounded serious. "You must decide. And then you must convince me. Because when all of this is done, you and I will not play little games of pretend that it was not something you wanted."

"I have no idea what to say to that," she said, which was true, but not for the reasons she thought he might suspect.

"You have no choice whether or not to be here, nor what will happen," Renzo said, his long fingers toying with his espresso cup before him in a way that made Sophie flush. "You will grow ever larger with my child. We will marry to give the child my name. These things cannot be avoided. But how you spend your time here before then? That is up to you."

"One choice," she whispered. "Lucky me."

Renzo looked at her then, and she was convinced he could see straight through her. That he could see every thought, every feeling, every shred of guilt she'd ever entertained. His dark amber gaze inhabited her. It set her on fire and threw gas on the flames.

And he didn't do anything but look.

"I have no doubt in my mind that you will be beneath me, spread out over my bed, begging for my touch," he told her, almost offhandedly. Though there was nothing *offhand* about the way he was looking at her. "Sooner rather than later, in fact. So I do hope that you enjoy this time, *cara mia*. It is the only power you have left."

"And here come those consequences again," she managed to say. She even sounded relatively calm, despite the fact she felt as if he had his hands wrapped tight around her and was wringing her limp. "I was just about to say we should do it. We should jump right in—maybe right here? But you had to be awful, again, and now I just don't know."

His mouth curved. Slowly. Much too slowly.

It was as if he wanted her to imagine those lips all over her naked body—and she did. That was the trouble. She really did.

"Tell yourself whatever lies you require to make yourself at peace with this decision," Renzo told her. "It will all end in the same place."

"You've made my mind up for me," she replied, and let her smile get a little sharper. "I'll just wander the halls for the next nine months like a flesh and blood ghost."

Renzo only laughed.

But Sophie wasn't kidding. She spent the day doing exactly that. She wandered the castle halls. She sat in the library and paged through more books, though she couldn't seem to concentrate on any of the words on the page. She walked down to the village and back. And all she could seem to think about were two words. *Mistress*, still. And *forgiveness*.

She couldn't help but think they were connected.

In the evening, she took her dinner in her room and stared at her mobile again. For a long time.

And then, before she could talk herself out of it, she wrote formal letters of apology to her parents and to Dal, because she owed them at least that much.

Her parents were not warm people, or at least not to her, but they had never wavered in the things they'd wanted and Sophie had meekly gone along with all of them. The only time she'd ever stood up for herself was the matter of her engagement. Her parents had never had the slightest inkling that Sophie wasn't happy. She'd never given them that courtesy.

And of course she knew that they wouldn't have reacted well even if she had told them. But she couldn't worry about their reactions now, she could only do what she felt was right. And running out on her own wedding, leaving them to sort it out in her wake, was a terrible thing to do to anyone.

She took responsibility for that.

Her letter to Dal was harder. She barely knew him, but that didn't change the fact that both of them had expected that they would marry each other, and had agreed to go ahead with it. And the fact he was remote and made entirely of ice, as far as she could tell, didn't change the fact that she'd made a promise to him and then broken it. First in Monaco and then, much more publicly, at Langston House.

When she hadn't fought to escape Renzo. If she was honest, his appearance had been a relief.

She didn't tell Dal any of that. He was a smart man and when her baby arrived, Sophie was certain he'd be more than capable of doing that math. What she did do was apologize for betraying him and humiliating him, then leaving him to pick up the pieces after she'd roared away in Renzo's car.

Sophie couldn't say she wished she'd married him after all, because she didn't. But she could, and did, tell him that she wished she hadn't let the mess of her personal life take center stage like that, and in full view of everyone they knew.

She didn't expect any replies, but when she put her mobile away again, she felt…lighter. Free, almost, in a way she never had before.

Later, she lay in her bed and stared at her canopy again. She thought about Monaco and she thought about her baby. She thought about that night before her wedding, out on that dark country road, and the deep and utter despair she'd felt when Renzo had driven off and left her there.

She remembered walking down that aisle with her father, her gaze locked on Dal there at the altar. She remembered the misery of each step. Her sheer panic at the prospect of having to give to Dal what she'd so happily and easily handed to Renzo.

And most of all she remembered what she'd felt when the doors had slammed open behind her and Renzo had appeared.

She let out a little gasp, alone in her bed.

Because it hadn't occurred to her until this moment that she was in love with him.

Heedlessly, recklessly, foolishly in love with him. It had happened too fast, right there in Monte Carlo, surrounded on all sides by so much glittering European wealth. It had happened the moment he'd stood there before her and asked why she was sad.

When he'd seen something in her no one else had ever noticed.

She'd told him she didn't believe in immolation and he'd set her on fire anyway.

And then he'd taught her she could feel things she'd had no idea were even possible.

She loved him. She'd never loved anything or anyone in all her life, but she loved Renzo. He was heat and light. He was sunshine. Even his fury excited her on some level—and more, she didn't retreat into frozen affront when he provoked her, the way she did with everything else. She fought back. She lost her cool.

He had thawed her out and she hadn't even realized she was melting, all this time.

And she found she could forgive herself for that. It didn't mean she wasn't accountable for the choices she'd made. She should have called off her wedding. She should have found Renzo the moment she knew she was pregnant and told him he was going to be a father. She never should have forged on with her wedding to Dal, much less tried to imagine ways she could pass her baby off as his.

She would have to live with the knowledge that

when pressed, she was the sort of woman who would do all of those things, and had.

The truth was, she'd never been in love before, and it had made her a little crazy. Love wasn't a factor in her world. It wasn't a part of the marriages she'd known all her life. She wasn't surprised, looking back, that she'd reacted to these overwhelming emotions with very little grace.

But she'd apologized. Her parents and Dal could accept her apologies or not—but that was up to them.

Here, now, she had other things to face.

She sat up in her bed and looked at that door that sat there on her wall like a taunt. The truth was, she didn't want to be Renzo's mistress. But she didn't see the point of locking herself away in this room, Rapunzel by her own hand, simply because he refused to offer her the things she really wanted.

When she hadn't even known what she wanted until today.

She'd wanted to be free and he'd set her free, and her reaction to that had been to blame him for it.

She'd wanted to lose her innocence on her own

terms and he'd done that—oh, how he'd done that—and she'd blamed him when she'd fallen pregnant. Sophie might have been a virgin, but she wasn't an idiot. She'd known that all those times he'd been inside her that night in Monaco he'd used protection...except that first time. And she hadn't stopped him. She hadn't even tried to stop him.

She seemed to expect Renzo to read her mind and intuit her feelings even when she was a mystery to herself. Sophie might not know a whole lot about love, but she was fairly certain that wasn't the definition.

And she might not want an arrangement, cold and clinical—but then, Renzo could use any words he liked. She knew how bright and hot he burned. If he was clinical about anything, she'd never seen it.

She could be his mistress, if that was what he wanted. She could love him just as much, and better yet, she could have him while she did. She could explore him every night. She could use these months to get to know the father of her child, the lover who'd blown up her life when she'd least expected it, the only man she'd ever loved or, she imagined, ever would.

All she had to do was walk to that door, pull it open, and surrender.

Renzo heard the door latch and assumed he was dreaming.

After all, he had this dream every night.

Tonight was like every other time he'd dreamed this exact same thing. The door pushed inward, very nearly soundless. And then Sophie appeared, exactly as he wanted to see her. Her thick chestnut hair tumbling down around her shoulders. One of the little gowns she liked to sleep in that he remembered with great fondness from that morning in England. Her long, gorgeous legs were exposed, and the hem of her gown flirted with her thighs as she moved. Even her feet were bare, and he found himself as obsessed as ever.

As if it were this woman's vulnerabilities that got to him the most. As if her beauty was secondary.

He knew the exact moment it dawned on him that this wasn't a dream after all.

It was when she paused there at the foot of his

bed, her brown eyes nearly filled with gold then, and more than that—uncertainty.

In his dreams she was bold. Daring.

But it was that uncertainty that had him jack-knifing up to sitting position, so he could hold that gaze of hers with his.

"You appear to be lost, *cara mia*."

He hadn't meant to sound like that. But he'd thought this was a dream and so his voice was scratchy with the sleep he needed, though he'd been wide-awake, as usual. Scratchy and gruff and too dark for the occasion, but he didn't take it back.

And she didn't seem to mind.

"I'm not lost," she said softly.

And the thing that rushed in him then wasn't as simple as victory. It was edged with triumph, to be sure, and it seemed to come from different parts of him at once. There was all that longing that he had begun to think would never be assuaged. There was that endless greed for her that made him despair of himself.

But more than that, he wanted his hands on her. As simple as that. It was almost as if he worried that she really was some kind of phantom and if he didn't grip her as hard as he could, she might disappear.

He was already moving when it occurred to him that he had never reacted this way to a woman in all his life. Renzo Crisanti was nothing if not sure of himself, particularly in the bedroom.

But this was Sophie.

And everything with Sophie had been different from the start, loath as he was to admit it to himself.

He rolled to stand beside the bed and then met her at the foot of it, and once there, he indulged himself. He wrapped his hand over the nape of her neck and pulled her even closer.

Renzo knew he could never dream anything as perfect as the feel of Sophie's skin beneath his palm. Or her scent, that soap she preferred and the hint of something muskier that he knew was her. All her.

"I thought you wanted me to beg," she said, those pretty eyes of hers still not as certain as he might have liked, but with a smile on her sweet mouth.

"I insist upon it."

"What does begging entail, then?" Her smile

deepened and he could feel it where he was hardest. And neediest. "I assumed it would require I get on my knees."

"That is always a good place to start," he said, expecting her to flinch at his boldness.

But instead, Renzo watched in a kind of stunned amazement as Sophie sank to her knees before him.

CHAPTER TEN

HIS CHEST WAS so tight it made it hard to breathe. And Renzo was so hard he had serious doubts that he would last more than a moment if Sophie actually did what it looked like she was about to do.

Though that didn't seem to matter much as she gazed up at him from where she knelt, that uncertainty in her gaze changing into something a whole lot more like delight.

"What do you know about pleasuring a man this way?" Renzo asked gruffly.

He already knew the answer. But he liked it very much when she responded as he expected.

"Nothing at all," she confessed, almost happily. "We didn't get to that."

He found his hands at her face, his thumbs gently stroking the satiny expanse between her cheeks and her temples.

"A shocking oversight," he murmured. "But I

want you too much, I think. I'm not at all certain I can allow you to play with me tonight."

Her delicate hands were on his thighs. She held his gaze as she slid them farther up, waiting until he hissed in a breath to stop.

Renzo had gone to bed naked, as was his custom. He couldn't decide, in this moment, if he regretted that choice or not. Or if, in fact, he was thrilled that she clearly didn't wish to listen to him.

"I'm here as your mistress," Sophie said softly, the glint of something mischievous in her gaze. "It is my duty to serve you, is it not?"

And she didn't wait for him to answer.

She tipped forward, lowered that mouth of hers, and licked him.

And Renzo was only a man. Not a very good one.

He leaned back against the foot of the bed, let his head fall back, and allowed her to do with him as she wished.

That she was inexperienced was immediately evident, but much like that night in Monaco, it only made it better.

Because she treated him like a wondrous discovery. She used her hands. Her mouth, lips, and tongue. And all of that blazed in him, brighter and hotter by the moment to match the sweet heat of her mouth, but what got to him most was her excitement.

The little noises she made, as if taking him this way built the same fires in her as it did in him.

And he didn't have it in him to pull back from the edge when she licked and sucked him straight over it.

But this was Sophie, the woman who seemed to have been put on this earth to match him sexually in every possible way, so all she did was drink him down as he emptied himself into her mouth.

He pulled out, a new and not entirely welcome sensation working its way through his gut.

It was another kick of the sort of shame he'd deny he was capable of feeling, he thought, as he looked down at her and saw only the top of her head. She'd settled back on her heels, one hand at her lips. He didn't understand why she brought these things out in him. These…*feelings.*

"I could have been more gentle," he began, stiffly.

But when she lifted her head again, he saw that she was smiling.

And it was as if something in him simply… broke wide-open.

He hauled her to her feet, then threw her down on his mattress. She laughed as she fell, but then he came down on top of her, and her laughter quickly turned to sheer fire and that wild delight that always arced between them. She wrapped her arms around him, he took her mouth, desperate. Determined.

Addicted.

He couldn't get the gown off of her lush body fast enough. He tossed it aside and discovered that she was even better than he'd remembered. That morning in England had been a taste, and had only whet his appetite for more. For this.

For her.

And while he knew on some level that he had all the time in the world tonight, he couldn't seem to slow himself down. He couldn't seem to control himself.

Instead, Renzo lost himself in her.

She had called herself his mistress. And there

was something in him that caught on that, even as the primitive side of him roared its approval.

And either way, he intended to slake his thirst at last.

He took his time, relearning every inch of her body. He lavished attention on her neck, that collarbone that fascinated him, and her delicate, surprisingly capable hands that he couldn't seem to get enough of feeling against his own skin. He focused on her gorgeous breasts, worshipping one hard nipple and then the other. He worked his way down to her abdomen, testing the shallowness of her navel and the faint swell that he knew was his child, and smiled when she squirmed beneath him.

He skirted that part of her he knew was as desperate for him as he was for her, and took his time learning those legs he'd spent far too much time admiring lately. All the way down one leg then up the other, then he flipped her over and tended to her back. The supple length of her spine. The swell of her hips and the endless intrigue of her rounded bottom, and then the dark secrets beneath.

By the time he turned her over again, she was limp.

And better still, she was begging.

Just as he'd promised she would. And in some distant part of his brain, Renzo knew that he'd expected the begging to be different, somehow. That he would feel exalted and she would be humbled.

But it wasn't like that at all.

"Please, Renzo," she whispered. *"Please."*

And he was the one who was humbled that he got to touch her like this. That he alone got to bring her to the brink again and again.

And that he alone ever would, he thought then, fierce and sure.

He settled himself between her legs, and then, finally, licked his way into her molten softness.

And for a while there was nothing but the way she writhed beneath him, lifting her hips to meet his mouth, his tongue, even the edge of his teeth.

When she fell apart, she sobbed.

But Renzo was only just beginning.

He crawled his way back up her body as she lay there, flushed and boneless.

Mine, he thought. *All mine.*

And if there was something in him that whispered that *mistress* wasn't the word he wanted when it came to Sophie—well. It was the word that would do for now. Because it had to do.

Because he'd told her it was what he wanted.

He reached between them and fit himself to her softness at last. As hard and as desperate as if she'd never taken the edge off at all.

Sophie's eyes fluttered open and her gaze met his, and he took that as a sign, sliding himself deep inside her.

He wanted it fast. A wild pounding that would toss them both straight into oblivion, but she shifted beneath him.

Her eyes were brown and entirely too gold. Her mouth was soft and something like vulnerable. She slid her arms around his neck and held him to her, and it wasn't oblivion Renzo wanted.

It was this.

Her.

It was a sweet, hot joining. His deep slide inside of her and the way she clutched at him, as if it could never be enough.

They could never be close enough. He could never be deep enough. She could never take enough.

But for what felt like forever, they tried.

And Renzo knew fire. He knew wild heat and the oblivion it caused.

But there was something secret here, in the dark of his room, with only the sound of their breathing to spur them on.

There was something sacred in the way she held him and the sounds she made, sweet whispers and now and again, his name.

This time, when they reach that edge, it was together.

And there was no oblivion at the end of it.

There was only bliss.

Once Sophie agreed to be his mistress, everything fell into place.

Two weeks later, Renzo stood in the suite of rooms that had been hers when she'd first arrived, impatient and not doing much to hide it.

He had long since had her moved into his bedroom with him, because there was no sense pretending she would ever sleep in another bed but his. Today he waited as the doctor's assistants set up their equipment, turning what had briefly been Sophie's room into a makeshift office.

"You look happy," the doctor said from beside him, in his jovial way. He clapped Renzo on the back. "Just as the proud papa should."

Renzo's first instinct was to deny it. He looked at the doctor, the only man in the village who had ever treated him or his mother with respect back in those dark years, and then he looked back at the bed, where Sophie was lying down. She had an easy smile on her face, and he seemed to be the only one having trouble with the knowledge that she was naked beneath the sheet spread over her lap.

Their days were filled with the hot Sicilian sun and sex, and Renzo could admit that he had never known anything quite like it.

He woke her in the mornings, well before the sky was lit. He took her fiercely then, tossing her from half-asleep into that wildfire they shared with his first deep thrust. They never spoke during those mad sessions. He left her limp and panting when he took his shower, then made his way down to his office to tend to his business concerns spread out across different time zones.

Hours later he met her for her breakfast, if business allowed.

He told her he needed to inspect the growing thickness in her belly, and he did, all over the castle—and then took advantage of the sweetness of his hands on her skin. He knew every part of her better than he knew his own body now, and he liked the taste of hers a good deal more.

Sometimes he knelt on the floor of the shower and licked her until she sobbed. Sometimes Sophie did the kneeling, proving to him what a quick learner she was every time she took him deeper into her mouth.

Other times he lifted her against the nearest wall and surged inside her, riding them both straight back into that bliss that only seemed to expand every time they reached it, wide and glorious.

It was hard to remember that when she'd arrived they hadn't had their evening meals together. Now Renzo insisted upon it. No matter what time he finished with his various business concerns, stuck on video calls all around the globe, Sophie waited for him. And they sat out on one of the terraces, eating and talking as the night grew deeper blue all around them and the summer sunset painted the sky.

Renzo learned that she was funny. That the poise and elegance she could draw around her like armor was an act, not the truth of her. Sometimes they argued books. Politics. World events and history. She knew proper Italian, so he taught her his Sicilian dialect and the filthy words and phrases he doubted very much anyone else had dared utter in the presence of the excruciatingly correct Carmichael-Jones heiress.

They talked until the stars came out and then he took her to his bed, where he got much more serious.

He was as demanding as he was creative, and Sophie was even better than he'd imagined she was in Monaco, when she had somehow managed to knock his whole world off its axis.

She matched him completely.

And the madness of it was, the more he had her, the more he wanted her.

As if there was no bottom to that hunger, the way there always had been with anything else he'd longed for. She was bottomless.

And she was having his child.

No matter how quickly he divorced her after she gave birth, those things would remain true.

"Impending fatherhood agrees with me," he said to the doctor now.

Because he couldn't quite bring himself to use the word that fit. *Happy.* He'd never imagined it was a word that could be applied to him. He'd never thought much about it either way. He'd survived his childhood. He'd survived his one and only attempt to make sense of how his father had treated his mother and him, but it had been a close call, and not one he cared to repeat.

And his response to his father's harsh welcome had been to make himself rich and famous instead of slinking off into the shadows to die of shame, as he'd clearly been meant to do.

Happiness had never seemed like much of a goal next to all that.

The doctor's assistants prepared Sophie, rolling the machines closer to her. But she was the one who lifted her head and beckoned for Renzo to come near. He did, standing awkwardly by the side of the bed, not knowing where to look.

And then not quite knowing what to do when Sophie took his hand as if it was the most natural thing in the world.

She made it entirely too easy to feel the kinds of things about her that he knew he shouldn't. He *couldn't.*

But he didn't have time, now, to worry about that.

Because there was an image on the monitor.

A tiny blob, curled around itself like a marvelous bean.

"Look," Sophie said softly. "It's our child."

Their child.

Renzo found himself holding on to Sophie's hand a little too hard as a hard swell of pure joy threatened to take out his knees.

And he bit his own lip before he called this woman what she was, what he dared not admit even to himself.

Not his mistress. Or not merely his mistress, en route to being the mother of his child and his wife—if not in that order.

But a miracle.

Sophie had just come back from a rambling walk one late afternoon when one of the castle staff, who largely left her to her own devices, rushed into the master bedroom.

She'd gotten used to it being Renzo who met her here and introduced her to all the delicious things people could do with slick soap and a whole lot of hot water.

She had to force herself to lock up her reaction

to the images tumbling through her head and concentrate on the woman before her.

"We must get you ready," she was saying briskly. "*Il capo* is taking you out tonight."

And it didn't occur to Sophie to argue. What *il capo* wanted, *il capo* got—and what Sophie had learned over the course of her time here was that the things Renzo wanted, she tended to love.

She stepped into the gown that was laid out for her when she got out of the shower, a flowing, deep blue affair with a high neck in front and no back. She let the woman craft her hair into a complicated chignon that looked simple and then handled her own cosmetics, using only a bit of mascara to darken her lashes and a slick of color on her lips. She strapped herself into a high, impractical pair of sandals that the woman presented to her, admiring the clean, obviously Milanese craftsmanship.

"You must hurry," her attendant chided her when Sophie spent a little too long looking at herself in her mirror, wondering when she'd started to glow like that. As if she'd been plugged into an outlet. "*Il capo* does not like to be kept waiting."

And Sophie smiled, because she knew that was not entirely true.

She walked out to the grand stairway and began to make her way toward the main floor of the castle. She was halfway down the steps when a man stepped out of the library and moved to the bottom of the stairs. Sophie knew who it was in an instant, of course. She didn't have to see his face.

This man was tattooed deep into her skin and fused deep into her bones. He was a part of her, and not only because their child grew bigger inside of her by the day.

She would recognize that lean, mouthwateringly athletic form anywhere. Renzo wore another one of his dark suits tonight that effortlessly enhanced his already astonishingly beautiful form. He was dark and gorgeous and her blood heated as she moved toward him.

He looked at her as if he already owned her.

Which made Sophie wish that he did. Not as a part of *an arrangement*. Not as a mistress. The trouble with having Renzo at all, which perhaps she'd known from that very first night, was that it was never enough. She wanted everything.

She wanted things she didn't know how to name.

But she knew better than to say such a thing to him. She knew better than to ruin what they had. She knew this man—this beautiful, complicated, proud man—would reject her feelings if she was ever foolish enough to mention them out loud.

She told him with her body, every chance she got. She loved him with her hands and her mouth and the place she burned for him the hottest. She loved him when they slept tangled together, breathing as one. She loved him on those dark, wild mornings when he was inside her as she woke, catapulting her over that deliriously sweet edge before she knew her own name.

She loved him in all the ways she could. The only way she could.

Tonight she loved him with a smile and the way she held on to his hand when he took it in his.

"Where are we going?" she asked.

"Trust me," Renzo said.

And she did.

She wasn't entirely sure when that had happened, either. Maybe it had been right around the time she'd stopped blaming him for doing what she hadn't had the courage to do herself. When she'd accepted that she should have been the one to stop her wedding and leave that life behind if she didn't want it—instead of passive-aggressively waiting for her sins to catch up to her as she walked down the aisle in that chapel.

But she didn't want to think about such things tonight. Not when Renzo was dressed to devastate, that deep fire she loved so much making his dark eyes gleam.

Another sleek, low-slung sports car waited for them out on the drive.

"How many cars do you have?" she asked him, but she was smiling.

Renzo opened her door for her and helped her in. "I like cars."

There was a time when she might have seen a statement like that as proof of his arrogance. But she knew him better now. He had told her stories of growing up in this village, with no heat in the winters. His mother had done whatever domestic work she could find to make ends meet, and Renzo had helped as soon as he was old enough.

She couldn't begrudge a man who'd grown up with a hollow belly every night the things he'd earned with his own hard work. The truth was, she thought as he drove them through the village, was that she couldn't find it in her to begrudge this man anything.

He took the single road out of the village, but instead of turning south toward Taormina, he headed in the opposite direction. It took Sophie a moment to understand that they were headed for the next ridge. And the hotel he'd built high above a sweeping vineyard.

Much like the castle, the hotel clung to the side of a cliff. It was all red roofs and golden light, bright against the evening. Renzo pulled up to the front of the main hotel building, and was greeted by name by the brace of valets waiting there.

But it wasn't only that they knew his name. They appeared to genuinely like him.

The same thing seemed true of every hotel employee they passed when they walked inside. They were deferential, certainly, but Sophie knew the difference between professional courtesy and genuine affection. This was the latter.

If she'd had any doubt that Renzo had done exactly what he claimed to do—that he'd really saved the village and everyone in it, along with himself—she thought this proved it.

Renzo led her through the main part of the hotel,

arranged on sumptuous levels to make the most of the views in all directions. Then he ushered her outside again, and up a path scented with night flowers and the distant sea toward a separate villa, higher up on the cliff.

Inside, the rooms were airy and let the mountains in. And dinner had been set for them out on the terrace that ran the length of the building.

Sophie stepped out into the sweet evening and looked out at the village she knew so well now, and beyond that, the castle where she'd lived all these weeks.

It felt like magic, but it paled next to the enchantment of the man who came and joined her at the rail.

"I'm not at all surprised that this hotel is successful," she said. "The village looks like something out of a fairy tale. Complete with a perfect castle."

"I don't believe in fairy tales," Renzo said. There was a set to his jaw that she hadn't seen in a while. Something very nearly belligerent—but in the next moment it was gone, and Sophie wondered if she'd imagined it. Especially when he smiled at her. "But as long as the guests do, that's all that matters."

There was a different charge in the air between them, Sophie thought as they sat at the pretty little table and ate dinner there under the stars. A darker, more insistent kind of electricity, and there was a knot of something like anticipation deep in her belly.

The food was exquisite. The Sicilian summer night was soft and beautiful. And the man across from her was far more stunning than any of their surroundings. Sophie thought she could happily gaze at him forever.

They sipped small cups of strong coffee after the last of the plates had been cleared away. And when she heard the hotel staff close the front door of the villa, Sophie expected Renzo to reach for her.

But he didn't.

Instead, he reached into the interior pocket of his suit jacket, and pulled something out. And before she could identify what it was, he stood from his seat, let his mouth curve into that sensual quirk that still drove her mad, and then pulled her up to stand with him there at the rail.

Her heart stopped beating. Then kicked, so hard it made her dizzy.

"What…what are you doing?"

"I think, *cara*, that you know very well I am not about to break into dance."

His sardonic tone felt like rich chocolate, thick and decadent, pouring all over her.

"I think I'd like to see you dance, now that you mention it."

"Alas, another dream that will never come true," Renzo murmured. His expression turned serious. "You told me that your engagement to your earl involved the signing of contracts in your father's office, did you not?"

"Yes." Sophie was beyond startled. She was… something else entirely, and she couldn't seem to get a handle on it. She could only answer his questions. "I was called in. Dal was already there and he and my father signed the papers. Then, some weeks later, there was a dinner."

"This is not a contract for your father to sign," Renzo told her then, gruff and serious. "This is a contract you wear yourself."

He presented the box he held to her and cracked it open.

It was a diamond ring that seemed to catch every bit of light and make it brighter. And Sophie hadn't given a lot of thought to the sort of diamond a man like Renzo might prefer, but she knew in an instant that if she had, it would not have been this one.

She would have expected something modern and edgy from him, to match the way he fused history and a contemporary sensibility in places like this hotel or the castle across the way. An emerald cut rectangle, perhaps, to show off the carats and express his domination.

But the ring he held before her looked like all the fairy tales he'd claimed he didn't believe in. Three round diamonds surrounded by pavé and filigree, suitable for princesses and storybooks alike.

It made her heart thud. And more, it told her things about Renzo she was positive he didn't know himself.

Like that intent fierceness in his gaze, as if he didn't know what her answer would be. As if he was in some doubt about this thing between them, though she knew he'd never admit he entertained uncertainty. Not when he'd been so clear about the progression. Mistress. Wife only long enough to provide legitimacy to his child. An engagement, complete with a ring, hadn't been part of it.

But she wasn't entirely sure he knew what she could see in him tonight, and that made her heart kick at her again. Harder than before.

Renzo's mouth was set in that stern line, as if what he expected from her was an argument. Because, she understood then, he had fought for everything he had. Everything.

Even her.

"Marry me," he said, more order than invitation, because that was who he was. The only man Sophie loved, or ever would. "Now."

CHAPTER ELEVEN

RENZO DIDN'T WAIT for Sophie to answer. He pulled the ring from the box and took her hand in his, sliding the astonishingly dreamy piece of jewelry onto her finger.

Where, Sophie couldn't help but notice, it fit perfectly.

As if it was meant to be there. As if *this* was what had been meant to happen all along, no matter what he'd told her.

And for a moment, everything disappeared. The island of Sicily was no more. There was no hotel, no rolling vineyards beneath the stars, no postcard-perfect village in the distance.

There was only this particular moment of communion. Special, sacred. A kind of holy she had only experienced before when he was deep inside her, and she was showing him how much she loved him with every touch.

This was like that. And yet more, somehow.

Sophie felt shaken. But not in a way that left her weak. She felt shaken and strong, somehow.

Right, a voice inside her intoned, like the ringing of a bell. *This is* right.

It was as if everything was finally right, at last. It all made sense. That night in Monte Carlo led straight to this. And every step along the way felt necessary. Important.

Their own kind of perfect.

"Yes, I'll marry you," Sophie said, and smiled to keep her emotions in check, though she wasn't sure she succeeded. "Not that you asked."

"I didn't realize it was a question that needed asking." But there was a curve to Renzo's beautiful mouth. And he still hadn't let go of her hand. "This was always the plan, was it not?"

And she loved him, so she didn't point out that bloodlessly cold arranged marriages rarely began with actual proposals like this one. She loved him, so she only smiled wider. She loved him, so she—

Sophie frowned, as all of his words finally penetrated. "Did you say *now*?"

Renzo kept his eyes on hers. That curve in his mouth became a true smile. And he lifted his free hand.

The staff that Sophie had thought gone reappeared then. And this time, they brought in a man wreathed in smiles who bowed, complimented *il capo* on the happy news, and introduced himself to Sophie as the mayor of the village.

"How is this possible?" she asked Renzo. "I thought weddings in Italy required…?"

"The mayor owes me a favor," Renzo replied, still holding her hand as if he thought she might make a break for it. "I rebuilt his house. In return he issued me a special marriage license, handled the paperwork, and posted the banns over the last weeks."

Sophie found she was breathless, but she couldn't quite bring herself to mind. "When you said *now*, you meant right now."

Renzo only looked at her, his dark amber eyes so fierce and consuming.

And in the end, it wasn't a struggle. Sophie was already in love with him. She was already carrying his baby. As far she was concerned, marrying him was nothing but a technicality.

She remembered what he'd said about their divorce and visitation rights—but she shoved it aside. That had been so long ago, now. She'd seen the look on his face when he'd looked at their baby on the ultrasound monitor. And tonight, as he'd given her the ring she wore.

Renzo might not say he loved her. He might not know that he did. But she was sure—she was more than sure—that there was no way she was in this deep alone.

And this time, there was no aisle to walk down and no second thoughts. They stood on the balcony with all the world sparkling there at their feet, and spoke their vows.

When Sophie promised to love and honor Renzo, she meant it.

And she thought he did, too.

When the simple ceremony was done, the staff made their exit and Renzo finally swept her up and into his arms. For a moment, he simply held her there.

She couldn't keep herself from reaching for him. She laid the hand that now sported the two rings he'd given her against his jaw, and wasn't certain her body could contain all the joy that pulsed in her then.

It was like that light in his eyes, fierce and encompassing.

"You married me," Sophie said softly, and she couldn't seem to stop smiling.

"I told you I would," Renzo replied, his voice low and his dark eyes aglow as he held her high against his chest. "I keep my promises, *cara*. You should know this about me."

"And your vows."

"Always."

He carried her into one of the villa's sumptuous bedchambers. The bed was a high, commanding platform strewn with rose petals, and Renzo carefully laid her down in the middle of them.

And then he worshipped her with his body. There was no other way to describe it.

In a kind of reverent silence, he slipped the shoes from her feet. He set his mouth and his hands to every centimeter of her body, claiming her and exalting her.

It was as if he was imprinting himself…everywhere. By the time he took her dress off, and stripped her down until she was wearing nothing but the rings he'd put on her finger, Sophie felt outside herself.

Almost sick with joy. Heavy with it.

She couldn't touch him enough. She couldn't kiss him, taste him, explore him enough.

She couldn't get *enough.*

Renzo was a man possessed. He ran his hands over her belly and the beginnings of her bump, murmuring praise and devotion to his child the way he always did.

But when it came to the rest of her, he'd clearly set himself the task of taking her apart.

And he did. Over and over and over again.

Sophie lost track of how many times she shattered on his fingers. His mouth.

And when he finally pulled her on top of him, holding her where he wanted her as he surged into her, she was too far gone to be careful. She was lost in the joy of this. The beauty that was this night, this man.

The exquisite wonder that was the light and hope they made between them.

She heard the sound of her voice, repeating something again and again, like a chant.

His hands gripped her hips, almost too hard for comfort, as he set an intense pace.

"Again," he ordered her, ferocious and commanding below her. "I want you to come again."

And when she didn't obey him immediately, he moved his clever fingers to her center, and pressed down hard.

Sophie shattered one more time. She thought she died, it went on so long, and the only thing she was aware of for a very long while was Renzo's hoarse shout as he followed her.

It felt like much later when she came back to herself, slumped on top of him as if he really had broken her.

And it took her longer than it should have to realize that he was not holding her the way he normally did. He was…tense, there below her, still inside her.

She would have said he was angry if they hadn't just—

But that was when she realized what she'd done. What she'd been repeating over and over again while out of her mind, hopped up on their impromptu wedding and these weeks of loving him with everything she had.

Over and over and over again, so there could be no mistake.

She could *hear* it, as if there was an echo in the room, beating her with her own words.

I love you, she'd said, fool that she was. She'd cried it out again and again. *I love you, I love you.*

Renzo, I love you.

She didn't want to open her eyes. She didn't want to face it when she could feel him beneath her, stiff and furious.

But that was the old Sophie. The one who'd walked halfway down an aisle toward a man she could never love and didn't even want because she'd imagined it was easier than causing a scene.

The new Sophie didn't hide from her problems. She didn't go along with things simply to avoid conflict, no matter how much she might want to do just that.

And she had never wanted to do it more than she did just then.

She forced herself to open her eyes and lift her head, facing Renzo straight on.

He was staring back at her, his dark amber eyes like a storm, his expression grim.

And she knew that everything had changed.

Again.

"You do not love me," Renzo bit out at her.

She was soft and much too sweet. He was still

deep inside her and all he could feel was that soft heat of hers, making him stir all over again. She was his wife.

His wife.

But that didn't matter. He couldn't let that matter.

Because all he could hear were those damned words. Those terrible, ruinous words.

He expected her to deny it. To wave it away, and the sad part was, he knew he would accept it if she did. He would choose to believe she'd been carried away. They'd had a wedding, after all, and this one hadn't been interrupted. She wore his rings and she'd made her pretty vows, making his child legitimate well before its birth, just as he'd always wanted.

If she told him she'd made a mistake, he would believe her.

He *wanted* to believe her, with a sharp-edged ferocity that made him feel something like dizzy.

But Sophie pushed herself up slowly, still straddling him, as if she could feel him all over her and deep inside her and *in her bones* the way he could feel her.

Her gaze was somber. Almost sad, and he had a terrible inkling—

"I'm sorry if it upsets you," she said, very quietly. Very distinctly. "But I do."

"I told you that was unacceptable from the start. Our arrangement—"

"It turns out that my heart doesn't care what arrangement we made," she replied, much too softly. And with that glowing thing in her melting brown eyes that he didn't want to identify. He didn't want to see it, because he knew it had been there awhile. He didn't want to admit to himself just how long. "And I think yours—"

"No."

He lifted her up and off of him. Then he was rolling out of the bed before he fully understood he meant to move. All he could think about was getting away from her. Getting away from *this*.

His worst nightmare come to life.

"Renzo—"

"You knew the rules. I told you the rules."

He didn't sound like himself. And that was the trouble, wasn't it? He hadn't been acting like himself for weeks. All this…domestic bliss, as if that was a real possibility for a man like him. What had he been playing at?

Renzo pulled his clothes back on in quick, determined jerks. Then he headed for the door, knowing nothing except he needed space. A hell of a lot of space. A continent or two, by his estimation.

He should have known better. He *had* known better. He'd known the moment he'd laid eyes on her in that casino that he should steer clear of her.

The trouble was, he had wanted Sophie too much.

The trouble was, he still did.

There had been so many warning signs and he'd ignored every one. This was supposed to be a punishment, not a love story. Because he could handle one.

The other was nothing but a lie—he knew that better than anyone.

He refused to handle this. He didn't even want to think about it.

He needed to get out of here.

"Renzo, please!"

When he looked over his shoulder, Sophie had pulled one of the bedsheets around her and was standing there in the center of the villa's spacious main room, her gaze imploring.

And he knew he would live the rest of his life and never manage to get this image of her out of his head. Her gorgeous hair tousled from his hands, hanging all around her. Her beautiful eyes, wide and hurt. That faint trembling he could see on her lips.

His beautiful Sophie. His wife.

"You need to leave Sicily immediately," he growled at her.

"Leave?" She swayed slightly on her feet and he didn't put out a hand to steady her. And he hated himself with a comprehensive ferocity that should have toppled him. And yet didn't. Somehow he was still standing. "Where will I go?"

"I have properties all over Europe. Any one of them will do."

He should never have brought her here in the first place. He understood that now, with the awful clarity of retrospect. There was too much of his old self here. That lonely outcast he'd been. That boy still full up on optimism and hope, in those long, cold years when he'd still imagined things could be different.

And more, that he could change them.

He'd been a fool then. He was a fool now. He should have known that he wouldn't be able to keep the two separate, the way they had been for almost the whole of his adult life. Not with a woman like Sophie.

Her smile was too pretty. It lit up parts of him he'd thought dead for more than a decade.

But Renzo didn't believe in resurrection.

"You said I would stay here for the duration of my pregnancy," she reminded him, clutching at that sheet as if it could save her from this. From him.

But it was too late for that. No one was getting saved here, least of all the woman he'd warned not to do the very thing she'd gone ahead and done.

"Now I'm saying that's unacceptable," he told her, cold and brutal. "You can't stay here another day."

"It doesn't change anything," she threw at him. "I've been in love with you this whole time. Don't you realize that? Do you really believe I would have just gone off with any man who smiled at me that night in Monte Carlo?"

"Stop," he ordered her, though his own voice sounded ragged. "Now."

"Of course not," Sophie said, answering her own question. And there was too much emotion—on her face, in her voice, filling up the villa. Filling up him, too. "It was you, Renzo. Only and ever you. I didn't ask you to love me back. I didn't ask you for anything."

He knew he didn't make a noise, and he didn't understand how, when everything inside him was a roar. A howl.

"You asked for everything," he gritted out at her, hardly knowing what he meant to say. "But I don't have it in me. I don't have anything to give."

"You do."

She stepped closer to him, proving that she was far more courageous than he'd ever given her credit for, and she even reached out as if she meant to touch him. And he wanted that touch. God, how he wanted it—almost as much as he wanted her to never, ever touch him with those hands of hers again, because he didn't think he could bear it.

But she stopped before she made contact.

And Renzo couldn't tell if he was happy about that or if it broke him.

"You do," she said again, more intently. "I know you do. I can feel it."

"Love is a vicious lie," he told her, and the words hurt him as they tore from his throat. "A delusion."

"Renzo—"

But he didn't stop. "I left this place when I was eighteen. You know that. I couldn't wait to go. What you don't know is that I didn't leave here to make money. All I wanted was to take care of my mother, at last. The way she'd always taken care of me."

"I think that's the very definition of love."

"She loved my father," Renzo told her. "She was the chambermaid in his great, grand palace in the Alps, and she loved him. He toyed with her, and she loved him. He brought home a wife, and still she loved him. And he let her because he liked it."

Sophie had dropped her hand back down to her side, but she didn't back away. And she didn't try to interrupt him again.

"Until she fell pregnant, that was, and then he kicked her out. With nothing." Renzo shook his head. "And she still loved him. She made excuses for him. He had duties, you see. Responsibilities. He couldn't help that he was swept up in events and promises beyond his control. Does that sound familiar?"

Sophie blanched at that, and Renzo hated himself all the more for drawing that line between his worthless father and his own, personal miracle.

But he didn't take it back.

"And when I was eighteen and finally a man grown in my estimation, I went to find him. This man who my mother still loved all those years later, when she had done nothing but suffer and raise me, destroying her own health in the process."

"Did you find him?"

Renzo's lips thinned. "My father is not a hard man to find. Access to him is another matter, of course." These were not pleasant memories, but he forced himself to spit them out. This story he had never told another living soul. "I had to present myself at his gates and petition for an audience. His men escorted me into his exalted presence. And I asked him why, if he'd loved my mother, he'd cast her—and me—aside."

He still remembered that day. Every excruciating detail. The principality his father ruled small and remote and like a little jewel, tucked out of reach. The palace like a fairy tale, high in the Alps.

And the man who'd sat in the desperately ornate hall and smirked when he saw Renzo, because they had the same eyes.

The same damned eyes.

"He laughed at me," Renzo told Sophie with the same old bitterness that had nearly killed him then. Some part of him thought it had. Because he had never been the same. "He laughed and he laughed. He called my mother names that I cannot repeat. And when I took a swing at him, he had his guards beat me."

Sophie only whispered his name, but he felt it like a touch. And he steeled himself to tell her the rest.

"When I was bloody, he told me to kneel," Renzo told her. "I declined. And so this man my mother still loved, my father, threw me into his prison. And left me there for a week."

He found Sophie's face, the only bright thing in the middle of all those dark memories.

But he didn't believe in brightness any more than he believed in love. Or hope.

"They dragged me before him again. And this time, he didn't laugh. He looked me in the eye and he warned me never to return." Renzo shook his head, trying to clear those nasty old memories. The viciousness on the older man's face. His total lack of concern about the things he'd done to his own child. "And when I returned here, somehow, my mother knew."

"What he did to you?"

"No. That I had found him. I never told her what he did." Renzo let out a laugh then, though there was little mirth in it. "And after eighteen years of no contact, do you know what she asked me? She wanted to know how he was. If *he* was okay." He found he still couldn't believe it. "Can you imagine?"

"She loved him," Sophie said simply.

Renzo was glad she did. It reminded him what was at stake here. What was happening when he should have known better than to allow it to come to this.

"I lied to her," Renzo told Sophie then. "I spun her a tale about a man trapped by his duty and unable to do right by her, because that was the story she'd told herself all those years. That was what she needed. And she was a sick old woman who had sacrificed too much for her folly, so she was happy to believe me. But I knew the truth. I knew that man was nothing. Less than nothing. He didn't deserve her love and he certainly didn't return it." He blew out a breath, surprised to find that wounds he'd thought he cauterized years ago still had the power to hurt him. "And I let my own mother die, believing this lie. That is the kind of man I am."

"I'm sure it gave her comfort to believe it," Sophie said with a kind of urgency in her voice, and too much emotion in her gaze. "There's nothing wrong with that."

"Love is a curse," Renzo told her, his voice nearly shaking from the force of his fury, black and terrible. "It is a poison. I told you not to fall in love with me, Sophie. I warned you." He stepped back, because he wanted to step forward and he didn't understand it. But he knew he couldn't allow it. "I warned you."

"Renzo."

She sounded wounded, and he hated it—but

there was nothing he could do. He knew what love did. It twisted and corroded. It was nothing but lies and it ended in blood on the floor of a distant jail cell and fairy tales his mother should have known better than to believe. He knew exactly what love was.

"What do you think will happen?" Sophie was asking, sounding as torn up as he was inside. "You can't possibly think—"

"Love is a sickness, nothing more," he threw at her, and it didn't matter how she looked at him. It didn't matter how he felt. What mattered was what he knew. What he'd had proven to him in no uncertain terms all those years ago. "You can love me all you want, Sophie. But you can do it alone."

And he left her there, his rings on her hand and his baby in her belly, because she'd given him no other choice.

Because leaving her might tear at him, more than he would have imagined possible and almost more than he could bear—but it was better than love.

CHAPTER TWELVE

FOR A LONG WHILE, Sophie stood where he had left her.

Right there in the middle of the villa, wearing nothing but a bedsheet. And her wedding rings.

She thought there was likely a joke in there somewhere, though she couldn't quite feel it. Not quite yet. Something about the bride who couldn't make it to the altar and the wife who couldn't make it through her wedding night.

Maybe someday she would find it funny.

She felt like an old woman by the time she finally moved, making her way into the shower though her bones ached and there was that horrible tightness in her chest she was afraid might never go away.

And Sophie stood in the hot spray and let the water course over her for a long, long time, as if it could wash her clean. As if it could rewind this evening to where it had all gone wrong.

As if it could allow her to start over and be a little wiser this time.

She didn't let herself fall apart. She didn't sob into the spray.

What would be the point? Renzo had already left.

When she finally emerged, she toweled herself off and tried not to pay any attention to the parts of her body that still seemed to hum, because longing for Renzo's touch was only going to make this worse.

Assuming it was possible that this could get worse.

She dressed herself in that same blue gown that Renzo had taken off of her so slowly, and swallowed hard against the lump in her throat. She combed her hair with her fingers and then gave it up as a lost cause—but then, she felt like one herself.

And when she stepped out into the main room of the villa again, there were hotel staff there waiting for her.

"*Il capo* has sent a car," the deferential man told her, inclining his head. The woman with him did the same. "If the *signora* would be so kind…"

Sophie tried to smile, but she hardly thought a grotesque twist of her lips did the job. She found she couldn't speak. She could only follow along as Renzo's people ushered her into a car that whisked her down the mountain.

Away from the village. Away from the castle she'd come to feel was like a home.

Away from Renzo.

The car delivered her to the airport in Catania, where a first-class ticket sat waiting for her. A quick flight to Rome tonight and then on to London in the morning.

He was sending her home.

Sophie took the ticket at the counter with fingers gone numb. Her driver had handed her a small folio containing her passport and credit cards when she'd gotten out of the car, as well as a small case. When she made it to her gate, still in a fog, she unzipped it and looked through it. It contained the few clothes Renzo had liberated from her honeymoon luggage back in Langston House, what felt like a lifetime ago, as if he was sending her back with only what she'd had when he'd taken her.

As if none of this had ever happened.

She closed the case and sat back. And then found herself looking at her hands. At the two rings Renzo had slid onto her fingers earlier tonight. The romantic fantasy in diamonds and with it, a platinum eternity band. Bright and shining, no matter what angle she looked at them from.

There was a kind of bubble in her chest, and Sophie was terribly afraid that it was filled with poison. And more, that if it burst it would destroy her.

But the longer she stared at the rings on her finger, the more that bubble…shifted.

Until Sophie was fairly certain it wasn't so much pain in there as a kind of wild fury.

The gate agent started boarding her flight, but Sophie didn't move.

She didn't want to go to back to London. She didn't want to be sent back to her parents' house, or wherever it was Renzo thought she would go once he was rid of her. There was nothing for her but scandal and pity in England, and Sophie very much doubted she'd want to deal with any of that at all, much less in a fashion that would please her family.

Why not just get on the plane? a voice inside

asked, sounding caustic and accusatory. *This is what you always do.*

And Sophie didn't disagree. Here she was, sitting in her deep blue wedding dress, her hair still damp and her heart smashed into pieces in her chest. Renzo had raged at her. His eyes had been dark with the past, and she had known without having to ask that he didn't see her—he saw his memories.

And so she had stood there, like that ghost she'd been so sure she was becoming, and she had done nothing but watch him leave.

Then she had simply acquiesced the way she always did.

She'd let them hustle her off that mountain. She'd taken her case and her passport without a word, and she'd obediently marched up to the ticket counter and accepted what amounted to an eviction notice.

The old Sophie would have already boarded the plane and sat there in her seat in a miserable little ball. She would have felt all the same heartache and anger that Sophie did right now, but she would have done what she'd been told to do anyway.

Because she'd always done what she'd been told to do.

But Renzo hadn't married the old Sophie. Renzo had pretty much wrecked the old Sophie. And then he'd gone ahead and married this one.

And *this* Sophie had absolutely no intention of shuffling off quietly into that dark night, simply because Renzo's feelings were hurt. Or because something in his past—even something as truly awful as the story he'd told her—had ruined him and made him think he couldn't feel things or love anyone.

Sophie knew a thing or two about ruin, as it happened. And what she'd learned most of all was that it was entirely up to her how ruined she chose to feel.

"Apologies, *signora*," the gate agent said then, snapping Sophie back to the Catania Airport. To the here and now and the choice she needed to make. "But the plane is fully boarded and ready to depart. If you would take your seat…?"

This time, when Sophie smiled, her lips worked the way they were meant to. She stood, gripping her case so hard in one hand she was surprised that the handle didn't break off.

"Thank you," she told the gate agent. "But I won't be getting on that plane."

She wasn't going to sit around and hope that

Renzo came to his senses. She wasn't going to meekly make her way back to England, and spend her life apologizing for something she wasn't all that sorry about to people whose opinions meant nothing to her.

She had told him that she loved him. And Sophie might not have had a whole lot of experience with love, it was true. But she knew it wasn't leaving when things were rough. She knew it wasn't taking hurtful words as gospel when she knew—*she knew*—that whether he was aware of it or not, Renzo loved her to distraction.

Because love was standing up for what she believed. Love was protecting her little family, the baby inside her and its beautiful, brooding, difficult father—especially when he didn't want her to do anything of the kind.

Renzo might not believe in love, but it was real and good whether he believed in it or not.

Sophie was simply going to have to show him.

When the door to his office in the castle opened, Renzo didn't look up.

He'd been going over reports in a kind of fever since the middle of the night, when he'd stopped pretending that he might get a moment's rest. He'd stared at his ceiling for a while, then decided that it was far better to immerse himself in work than lie in the bed he no longer shared with Sophie, imagining her with him. Beside him and below him.

But the change of venue hadn't helped.

There was no part of this castle he'd restored with his own two hands that didn't remind him of her. There was no escape. She was everywhere. He found himself listening for her step in the hall. He was sure he could still catch her scent in the air. And meanwhile, he felt disfigured by the things he had told her and more, the love she claimed to feel.

I love you, she had said, her head tipped back and her face awash in bliss. *I love you, Renzo. I love you.*

He would rather be in that prison again. He would rather have every bone in his body broken, repeatedly.

He would rather anything but this.

"It is not like you to hide, Renzo. Or to pretend that you are alone in this room when you must know very well you are not."

Sophie.

Renzo took his time raising his head. He wanted to believe that she was nothing but a ghost, but he knew better. She was too alive, there before him. Flushed and fierce, her hair in a glorious tangle and her hands on her hips. She still wore the blue dress he'd had made especially for her, and that nicked something in him.

Like a sharp blade pressed against his flesh.

There were too many things inside of him, then. Something like panic, harsh and suffocating. That same fire that only seemed to grow the longer he knew her, the flames dancing all over him the way her fingers might.

And in and around all of that, fury.

The same fury that had animated him all these lonely years. The fury he'd felt when he'd buried his mother, her ears still ringing from the lies he had told. The fury that had made him famous and then rich, because it had been what fueled him. It had been his favorite companion, down deep beneath the charm he wielded as a distraction or the laziness he assumed as a disguise.

It was the engine that drove him. It was all he'd ever thought he wanted.

Until Sophie had burst over him like a sunrise,

making him something other than the weapon he'd made himself into over that long week in his father's prison.

He had been a thing of fury and fire, but she had made him flesh.

Renzo had forgiven her the lies she'd told him, though he hadn't intended to do such a thing. It had happened sometime in these last weeks, a simple shift he'd only noticed after it had happened. He'd even forgiven her that ill-considered walk down an English aisle.

But this was the thing he couldn't—wouldn't—forgive.

"You are meant to be on a plane," he told her, his voice cold. "You should have landed in Rome already."

"It turns out that I don't really care for Rome at this time of year," she told him, and Renzo took an instant dislike to her tone.

She was too calm. Much too composed.

And the hectic glitter he could see in her dark eyes didn't assuage him.

"You have no business here," he said, clipped and chilly. "I told you to leave. I meant it."

"And if I were your mistress, I might obey you."

Her gaze met his, bold and defiant, and he hated that it took his breath. Still. “After all, what is a mistress if not a business arrangement? Intimate, perhaps, but never emotional. Isn’t that what you told me?”

“You know where the door is.”

Sophie’s lovely mouth curved. “Unfortunately for you, Renzo, I am not your mistress. I am your wife.”

He didn’t like that at all. “A situation that can be easily remedied.”

“Can it? Not for months, not if you wish your child to be born with your name.” She had the gall to let her smile widen when he scowled at her. “Oh, I’m sorry. Did you expect me to simply slink away, tail between my legs, in a shroud of shame for daring to express my feelings?”

Renzo didn’t know he’d shot to his feet, but there he was. Standing up, his hands and fists, and this maddening woman right there before him on the other side of his desk. Taunting him. Making him wish—

But no. The mistake he had made was in letting all of this go too far already. He should have sent her off to one of his other hotels in the first place. Somewhere faraway, where he could have had her pregnancy monitored by medical personnel, and never subject himself to this.

This terrible intimacy that felt like some kind of arthritis, making his bones protest.

"I can't imagine what you think this will accomplish," he told her, making a herculean effort to sound at least as calm as she did. "You're not going to argue me into changing my mind. I told you from the start what was between us. I regret that you got the wrong idea." He lifted a shoulder, then dropped it, in an excellent approximation of the ease that had been second nature to him before her. "I did warn you."

"The issue isn't whether or not I love you." Sophie sounded certain of that. "You asked me to be your mistress because you claimed that too many women, if left to their own devices, fell in love with you. That was why we needed the structure. That was why you insisted on our arrangement."

"And you shouldn't have broken the rules."

"I don't think the rules were in place to keep me from falling in love with you," she said gently, as if she was trying to explain astrophysics to a toddler. "You are so certain it was inevitable that you must have expected nothing less. I think you set those rules so that when it happened, you could gently disengage yourself and remind me what we'd agreed." She shook her head, almost as if she was sad. "But instead, you married me. Not as I was heading into childbirth, as threatened. But now."

Renzo didn't like the way that hit him, like some kind of indictment.

"That was always part of the plan. I told you not to read too much into it."

It was Sophie's turn to shrug and it set his teeth on edge.

"It turns out I'm terribly emotional," she said, much too offhandedly for Renzo's taste. "I can't help it. But what about you?"

He felt as if she'd shoved a stake through his heart. Part of him wished she had. It would be simpler. Cleaner.

"I don't know what you mean."

"I would be happy to apologize for the terrible sin of falling in love with you," she said quietly. "But first I want you to admit what we both know is the real truth."

When he only stared at her, she lifted her brows,

looking every inch the aristocratic Carmichael-Jones heiress.

His Sophie.

His wife.

"You're in love with me, Renzo," she said.

He was gripped by something he couldn't understand, then. He didn't know its name. It held on to him, like iron fists around his throat, his chest, his gut. It clenched hard, ripping the air from his lungs. Ripping him apart, but not fast enough.

Because he was still standing. He was still breathing.

And worst of all, Sophie was studying him as he stood there, filled with all this rage and need and fury and darkness.

He had the terrible feeling she could see all of it.

That it was possible she always had.

"I am not capable of love," he heard himself say, like rocks scraped together. "It is not in me."

"I know it is."

Her voice was so sure. So offensively *certain*. Renzo wanted to rage at her. He wanted to tear something apart, with his fingers if necessary, but he didn't let himself move. And even so, he felt as if the thing torn most was him.

“Then you have not heard a single thing I have ever told you,” he said, through his teeth.

“Renzo.” And he told himself he hated the way she said his name. As if it was a part of her. “You told me a story last night. About love.”

“I told you a story about doomed, damned men and the miseries they inflict on everyone around them. If that is not what you heard, then you have too many fairy tales on the brain.”

“You told me the story of a boy who was raised on a love story,” she corrected him.

“I told you about a boy who was raised on a *lie*, Sophie.”

“He had nothing,” Sophie continued as if she hadn’t heard him. “Except hope. And he took that hope and went to find the truth of the story he’d lived with all those years.”

“And that went so well. Hope blooms in prison, of course.”

“Your father sounds like an awful man. He beat you, but he didn’t break you. You came back here, and you could have passed on the kind of beating he gave you. You could have ripped out your mother’s heart and stamped it into the ground.”

Sophie's eyes were shining in a way that made him…ache. "But you didn't."

"You are telling me a story of weakness," Renzo snarled at her. "Why would anyone want to hear it?"

"You cared so much for her that you let her die believing in that love, when you knew it wasn't true." Sophie lifted her hands in a kind of supplication. "I can't think of a greater love than that. I only hope that you love our child so much, that you would protect it from everything, even itself."

He wanted to rage at that, but he couldn't seem to speak.

"You love me, Renzo, and you love this child," Sophie said, every word a blow. "And I know that you have no desire to be the kind of father yours was. Distant. Damaged. Do you?"

There was that howling thing inside of him, more complicated than simple fury. It was like a hurricane beneath his own skin, tearing him apart from his bones on out.

"You have to go," he managed to grit out.

But she didn't seem to hear him. Or she didn't care. She certainly didn't turn and leave as commanded. Instead, she moved toward him. Renzo stood as if he was frozen into place as she rounded the desk.

"You love me," she said again, more fervently this time. "You love our child. The only one you don't love, as far as I can tell, is you."

And he was cracking wide-open. He was a hurricane, or he was consumed by one, and he couldn't tell the difference.

The world was a howling thing, desperate and deadly, and Renzo didn't know how to fight it. He was known for his steadiness, and yet he felt rocked straight through. Her melting brown eyes, shot through with gold, were filled with something he didn't want to identify.

He didn't want to feel any of this. He didn't want to *feel*.

Sophie reached over and took his hand in hers. His fingers dwarfed hers, but she held it between the two of hers, and it took him a moment to realize that she was holding the hand where he wore a wedding ring to match hers.

"If you don't love yourself, that's all right," Sophie told him, the faintest tremor in her voice, as if these words were wrenched from her soul. "I can love you until you learn. I can love you forever, Renzo. I feel as if I already have."

And maybe it wasn't her vulnerabilities that he was so obsessed with, he thought in some distant part of his head that was still functioning. Maybe it was that she saw his, and loved him anyway.

Maybe all of this was love.

Maybe it always had been.

And Renzo had learned a long time ago to lean into the curves, the sharper and more treacherous, the better.

He didn't think it through. He'd already thought too much and it had brought him nothing but hurricanes and loneliness, and the truth was, he was tired of both. He shifted so that he held both of her hands.

And then, his gaze locked to hers, he sank to his knees before her.

He had never knelt before anyone or anything. But he knelt before Sophie.

"I don't know how to do this," he told her with every part of his battered, furious heart right there, exposed and open. "I buy things. I wait. I possess them. That is all I know."

She pulled her hands from his, and he felt it like

a loss. But she was only moving closer, so she could smooth her palms over his jaw, and sink her fingers into his hair.

"Do you think you are the only one who is new to this?" she demanded, a catch in her throat. "Did you hear a single word I said about the way I was raised? My parents may love something, but it isn't me. And I have never loved anything in all my life except you."

"Ah, Sophie. But I am not a good bet."

"Says the man I met in Monte Carlo," she said, her lips curving into the kind of smile he wanted to take with him and hold forever in his heart.

He shook his head, but her fingers moved as if she was trying to soothe him. As if he truly was a wild beast—but if he was, he saw she loved that, too.

It was written all over her.

"You deserve love, Renzo," she whispered. "You don't have to do anything. You don't have to tell me stories. You don't have to protect me from lies. All you have to do is let me love you. And let yourself love me in return. Everything else will work out."

Renzo wanted to believe it. He wanted it more

than he could remember wanting anything, even the father he'd longed to find so long ago.

"How do you know?" he demanded. "How can you possibly know?"

"Because those are the vows we made," she told him solemnly, her gaze on his. "We promised to love each other, even when it's hard. Especially when it's hard. It's easy to marry for the wrong reasons. It's easy to sign a contract and make it a business venture. It's easy to make arrangements and keep emotions out of things." He was gripping her hips as if he would never let go. And Sophie didn't look away. He wasn't sure she even blinked. "This is the hard stuff, Renzo. This is where the promises really count. Anyone can stay married when they have nothing to lose but a house. Or some money. But this? Loving you means fighting for you. The same way you would fight for me. Even if it hurts. *Especially* when it hurts. Or what's the point?"

Still kneeling before her, Renzo reached up to pull her face closer to his.

"I have never believed in love," he told her, in the way he'd said his wedding vows the night before. Deliberate. Considered. Like a contract signed in blood. "But I believe in you. I've tried so hard to let you go, to make you matter less—but here you are. I've tried and I've tried, but I can't quench my thirst for you. It only grows." Her gaze was too shiny again, and Renzo pushed on. "I want you below me. Beside me. I want you every way I've had you and a thousand ways I have yet to imagine. I want to watch you mother our child. I never know what you'll say, and I still want to hear every word. I want everything, Sophie. *Everything.* I don't know what this is."

"You do," she whispered. "You know you do."

"Promise me," he gritted out. "Promise me that you will always fight for me. For us. Even if you must fight *me* for us. And I will do the same."

"Renzo," she whispered, her lips curving as she spoke. "You tried to send me back to England. But here I am, high on a mountain in Sicily, right where I belong. You couldn't keep me from fighting for you. You can't."

"I will hold you to that," Renzo said, sure he sounded as broken as he felt.

And then he took her mouth with his.

And he was whole.

Renzo hadn't believed in love before he met her,

but she did. So he poured the things she'd taught him into his kiss.

All the longing. All the need.

The beauty of her smile that could light up any darkness, even his own heart. The magic of her laughter, that had healed him in ways he hadn't known he was broken.

He kissed her for all the fairy tales he'd never believed in, and the story she'd told him about his own life that made him want to believe in a good tale well told, with a happy ending after all.

Just so long as it was with her.

He would learn to love her if it killed him, he told himself. He suspected he already did.

And either way, she would never spend another moment questioning his devotion to her.

He was Renzo Crisanti. If there was a happy ending to be found, he would find it. And he would give it to Sophie, who had made him believe in forever.

And he was a man who kept his vows.

So that was what he did.

Alceu Cabbrieli Crisanti came into the world as if he was in a race, like his father. On his own schedule, a good two weeks before expected, with all the intensity and fury that Sophie supposed she should have expected from a child made by a man like Renzo.

And she loved him, red faced and angry-fisted, with a kind of ferocity that would have scared her a little, had Renzo not had the same expression on his face every time he looked at the child they'd made.

"My beautiful son," he would murmur, holding the fussing baby when he woke while Sophie prepared herself to feed him. And then, when Alceu latched onto her breast, Renzo would raise that darkly wondering gaze to hers. "My beautiful wife."

"Our family," she would say, as if it was a prayer.

It felt like a benediction.

They had spent a kind of honeymoon together these last months, waiting for Alceu's arrival. For a long time they'd kept the world out, but Sophie had known that was a state of affairs that couldn't last forever. No matter how she wished it could.

"Why can't it?" Renzo asked at the start of her final trimester. He had been lounging beside her in their bed, his hands on her belly to feel the baby kick inside her. "What do we owe the world?"

"This isn't about us," she'd told him, aware that he trusted her more by the day—but that it was still a battle. That his past was always with him.

That some things would take time.

And by the time the baby was born, she'd managed to convince her strong, proud, happily fierce Sicilian husband that it was worth his time to extend an olive branch to her parents. Or to suffer it while she did, more like.

"The truth is that it will cost you nothing," she told him after she'd made the initial phone call. "They will visit rarely, if at all. In the unlikely event they do, it will be as if they are miles away when they're in the same room. None of that matters."

"Then why bother?"

She'd stroked his lean jaw and marveled at the blaze in those dark amber eyes she loved so much. The blaze that was theirs. The blaze that had been there since the moment they'd clapped eyes on each other in Monaco and would be there when they were tottery and old.

Sophie and this man who still considered himself as solitary as the castle he'd rebuilt himself, even if he'd let her in. This man she was making a family with, making him less solitary by the day.

"Because they are going to be the grandparents of this child," she told him softly. "Whether you like it or not."

"I think it is you who do not like it, *cara*."

"The family business has to be run by someone," she said, raising her brows at him. "You fought for everything you have. Will you insist your son do the same?"

He answered her in his favorite way, with his mouth to hers, stoking that fire that only ever grew between them.

Which was as close to surrender as Renzo ever came.

Though on this particular sparkling day at the start of a Sicilian spring, Sophie thought that there were many different forms of surrender, and most of them looked like love.

Because today was Alceu's christening, in splendid Sicilian fashion. The lovely old church in the village had been ringing its bells all morning, and all that remained was for *il capo* and his little family to walk across the square to begin the mass.

"We will discuss consequences tonight," Renzo

told her as they walked. He held his son against his chest the way he liked to do, and Sophie marveled at the way the Sicilian sun made the pair of them glow.

As if love lit them up from all around.

"You do love your consequences," she murmured, laughing at him when he arched one of his king-of-the-universe looks her way. "Unfortunately for you, so do I."

"I believe I deserve sainthood for what I am about to endure. I may take it up with the priest."

"Poppy is my oldest and best friend," Sophie said, the way she had a hundred times already—today alone. "There can be no other possible choice for Alceu's godmother."

"And why that means the man you nearly married while pregnant with my son must also be involved, I do not know," Renzo retorted.

"Because he's Poppy's husband, as you are well aware." She smiled at him, ignoring his dark expression. "And he was never cruel to me, Renzo. It was quite the opposite."

She could see them up ahead, her best friend and the man Sophie had been supposed to marry. They waited out on the steps of the church, smiling at each other in a way that told Sophie without a single doubt that all of this had been meant to be.

Poppy and Dal never would have found each other in this way if Dal and Sophie had married. This Sophie knew for a fact.

And Sophie knew that she and Dal would never have looked at each other the way Poppy and Dal did. It was as if a warm current wrapped around the two of them and gleamed bright. As if they were connected whether or not they touched.

The fact that they were wildly, madly in love seemed to add an extra glow to the light dancing all over the square.

Not to mention, it made Sophie's heart feel three sizes too big.

Dal had accepted Sophie's apology. Poppy and Sophie had caught up at last—each with quite a story to tell.

And now Poppy and Dal would stand up with Sophie and Renzo and pledge to take care of the precious life they'd all had a hand in making, one way or another. Or maybe it was the other way around—Alceu was the life that had given them the courage or impetus to live the lives they'd been meant to live, not the lives they'd thought they were supposed to live.

Last June, on that bright morning outside of Winchester, could any of them have imagined they'd end up here? Much less so happy?

"Nonetheless," Renzo was saying in that low, dark, thrilling way of his that still made Sophie shiver in delight, "there will be hell to pay. Naked hell, *cara mia*, I hope it goes without saying. It is because I love you that I must punish you in this way, you understand."

"I love your punishments." She smiled at him. "And you. Always you."

Renzo held the back of his son's head in his hand as if there was nothing on earth more precious, and the smile he aimed at Sophie was filled with too much love to bear and a thousand promises, sex and devotion, honor and beauty, always.

She couldn't wait to live their whole, long, beautiful life together.

Because Sophie was a woman who kept her promises, especially to Renzo.

Each and every promise, as long as they both lived.

So that was precisely what she did.

Forever.

* * * * *